"Showcases the same astute and penetrating intelligence that characterized [Nguyen's] Pulitzer Prize-winning novel *The Sympathizer* . . . confirms Nguyen as an agile, trenchant writer." —*Seattle Times*

"These stories of Vietnamese refugees cast a lingering spell . . . [A] superb new collection." —*New York Times Book Review*

"Our first major Vietnamese-American writer, Nguyen is a prodigious genius making up for lost time." —*Newsday*

"Barbed with subtle humor that is wry and painful . . . beautiful . . . casts a formidable spell." —*Los Angeles Times*

"A necessary voice . . . stories as an act of resilience and survival . . . A beautifully written collection, filled with empathy and insight." —*Dallas Morning News*

"The perfect book to read at this historical moment in America . . . Nguyen takes readers deep inside his characters in a mere few pages . . . Read it now, or read it later but read it." —*Huffington Post*

Praise for *The Refugees*

"Viet Thanh Nguyen [is] one of our great chroniclers of displacement . . . Nguyen's narrative style—restrained, spare, avoiding metaphor or the syntactical virtuosity on display in every paragraph of *The Sympathizer*—is well suited for portraying tentative states . . . all Nguyen's fiction is pervaded by a shared intensity of vision, by stinging perceptions that drift like windblown ashes."
—Joyce Carol Oates, *New Yorker*

"Tragically good timing . . . A short-story collection mostly plumbing the experience of boat-bound Vietnamese who escaped to California . . . But there are others of different nationalities, alienated not from a nation but from love or home, and displaced in subtler ways . . . Ultimately, Nguyen enlarges empathy, the high ideal of literature and the enemy of hate and fear."   —Boris Kachka, *New York Magazine*

"In *The Refugees*, such figures aren't, contra Trump, an undifferentiated, threatening mass. They are complicatedly human and deserving our care and empathy . . . In our moment, to look faithfully and empathetically at the scars made by dislocation, to bear witness to the past pain and present vulnerability such scars speak of, is itself a political act."   —Anthony Domestico, *Boston Globe*

"The 2016 Pulitzer Prize winner returns with a beautifully crafted collection that explores the netherworld of Vietnamese refugees, whose lives and cultural dislocation he dissects with precision and grace."   —*O Magazine*

"A terrific new book of short stories . . . Nguyen is an exceptional storyteller who packs an enormous amount of information and images into a short work."   —Trine Tsouderos, *Chicago Tribune*

"The book we need now . . . demonstrates the richness of the refugee experience—and highlights its singular traumas . . . The most timely short story collection in recent memory . . . The stories in *The Refugees* [are] haunting and heart-wrenching, but also wry and unapologetic in their humanity."   —Doree Shafrir, *BuzzFeed*

"[A] quietly profound peek into the lives of Vietnam's deracinated and dispossessed . . . Absorb[s] both the nostalgia and bitterness that have characterized so many refugees in the decades since 1975."
—Rayyan Al-Shawaf, *San Francisco Chronicle*

"*The Refugees* is full of complicated family dynamics, cultural rifts and surprising resolutions . . . The eight unpredictable and moving stories that make up *The Refugees* are a remarkable achievement."
—Tom Zelman, *Minneapolis Star Tribune*

"[A] haunting and timely short story collection . . . These are stories worth meditation, each an arresting glimpse into the enduring disruption of flight and relocation."
—Julia Oller, *Columbus Dispatch*

"Despite the many accolades heaped upon Nguyen . . . it still comes as a revelation just how beguiling these stories are. Sharp, sardonic, poignant and profoundly human . . . The true power of this collection lies in the way Nguyen subverts stereotypical notions of the refugee experience, both sharpening and stretching our appreciation of its vast, universal dimensions in stories that range across generations, gender and time."   —Bron Sibree, *South China Morning Post*

"*The Refugees* will haunt its readers, especially in these times, when refugee stories need to be told, shared, and told again, ad infinitum."
—Rien Fertel, *A.V. Club*

"[A] sophisticated collection . . . Many of these short stories are bona fide perfect . . . Each story is so smooth that you don't at first realize how richly the author is layering his worlds . . . Nguyen's character studies are languorous and spacious, a collection that feels like a whole."   —*Saturday Paper*

"In the US, two kinds of stories typically exist about Vietnam and its people: jungles and napalm, or protest and politics. A new collection of short stories by Viet Thanh Nguyen will change that . . . Nguyen . . . is an expert on the implications of displacement . . . A worthy reminder that refugees are children, mothers, and fathers— not just casualties."   —Thu-Huong Ha, *Quartz*

"Nguyen's writing is lyrical and searingly evocative . . . An essential read for anyone seeking to understand the immigrant experience . . . Nguyen's writing as polished and powerful as it was in *The Sympathizer*—confirms the author's place among today's most compelling literary voices."   —Lien E. Le, *Harvard Crimson*

"The stories abound with images of doubleness and surreal twists of perception, often imbuing the narratives with a dreamlike clarity and strangeness . . . Throughout the collection Nguyen crafts a personal language and imagery superbly fitted to each character's volatile, near-inexpressible memories and reflections."   —James Grainger, *Toronto Star*

"With anger but not despair, with reconciliation but not unrealistic hope, and with genuine humor that is not used to diminish anyone, Nguyen has breathed life into many unforgettable characters, and given us a timely book focusing, in the words of Willa Cather, on 'the slow working out of fate in people of allied sentiment and allied blood.'"   —Yiyun Li, *Guardian*

"Delicately captures the traumas and triumphs of the migrant experience . . . Nguyen's stories are to be admired for their ability to encompass not only the trauma of forced migration but also the grand themes of identity, the complications of love and sexuality, and the general awkwardness of being . . . Nguyen writes . . . with a unique poetry."   —Fatima Bhutto, *Financial Times* (UK)

"This stunning collection of stories affirms the brilliance of Nguyen . . . A collection of exceptional stories that ring with topicality and truth . . . *The Refugees* is a book that needs to be read: it is astonishingly good."   —Donal O'Donoghue, *RTÉ Guide* (Ireland)

"A timely look at lives of outsiders in America . . . [Nguyen's] understanding of the refugee tragedy . . . is profound. Yet, the abiding power of these intelligent, crafted stories is his reading of human nature in domestic situations and often astute dialogue . . . [An] unpretentious, deliberate and well-observed collection."   —Eileen Battersby, *Irish Times*

THE REFUGEES

VIET THANH NGUYEN

Grove Press
New York

Versions of the stories collected here were originally published in the following publications: "Black-Eyed Women," in *Epoch*, 64.2; "The Other Man" (published as "A Correct Life"), in *Best New American Voices 2007*; "War Years," (published as "The War Years") in *TriQuarterly*, 135/136; "The Transplant" (published as "Arthur Arellano"), in *Narrative*, Spring 2010; "I'd Love You to Want Me" (published as "The Other Woman"), in *Gulf Coast*, 20.1; "The Americans," in the *Chicago Tribune*, December 2010; "Someone Else Besides You," in *Narrative*, Winter 2008; "Fatherland," in *Narrative*, Spring 2011.

Published simultaneously in Canada
Printed in the United States of America

First Grove Atlantic hardcover edition: February 2017
First Grove Atlantic paperback edition: January 2018

ISBN 978-0-8021-2736-5
eISBN 978-0-8021-8935-6

Library of Congress Cataloging-in-Publication data is available for this title.

Grove Press
an imprint of Grove Atlantic
154 West 14th Street
New York, NY 10011

Distributed by Publishers Group West

groveatlantic.com

18 19 20 21   10 9 8 7 6 5 4 3 2 1

For all refugees, everywhere

Contents

I wrote this book for the ghosts, who, because
they're outside of time, are the only ones with time.

Roberto Bolaño, *Antwerp*

It is not your memories which haunt you.
It is not what you have written down.
It is what you have forgotten, what you must forget.
What you must go on forgetting all your life.

James Fenton, "A German Requiem"

THE
REFUGEES

BLACK-EYED WOMEN

*F*ame would strike someone, usually the kind that healthy-minded people would not wish upon themselves, such as being kidnapped and kept prisoner for years, suffering humiliation in a sex scandal, or surviving something typically fatal. These survivors needed someone to help write their memoirs, and their agents might eventually come across me. "At least your name's not on anything," my mother once said. When I mentioned that I would not mind being thanked in the acknowledgments, she said, "Let me tell you a story." It would be the first time I heard this story, but not the last. "In our homeland," she went on, "there was a reporter who said the government tortured the people in prison. So the government does to him exactly what he said they did to others. They send him away and no one ever sees him again. That's what happens to writers who put their names on things."

By the time Victor Devoto chose me, I had resigned my-self to being one of those writers whose names did not appear on book covers. His agent had given him a book that I had ghostwritten, its ostensible author the father of a boy who had shot and killed several people at his school. "I identify with the father's guilt," Victor said to me. He was the sole survivor of an airplane crash, one hundred and seventy-three others having perished, including his wife and children. What was left of him appeared on all the talk shows, his body there but not much else. The voice was a soft monotone, and the eyes, on the occasions when they looked up, seemed to hold within them the silhouettes of mournful people. His publisher said that it was urgent that he finish his story while audiences still remembered the tragedy, and this was my preoccupation on the day my dead brother returned to me.

My mother woke me while it was still dark outside and said, "Don't be afraid."

Through my open door, the light from the hallway stung. "Why would I be afraid?"

When she said my brother's name, I did not think of my brother. He had died long ago. I closed my eyes and said I did not know anyone by that name, but she persisted. "He's here to see us," she said, stripping off my covers and tugging at me until I rose, eyes half-shut. She was sixty-three, moder-ately forgetful, and when she led me to the living room and cried out, I was not surprised. "He was right here," she said, kneeling by her floral armchair as she felt the carpet. "It's wet." She crawled to the front door in her cotton pajamas, following the trail. When I touched the carpet, it was damp. For a moment I twitched in belief, and the silence of the house at four in the morning felt ominous. Then I noticed the sound of rainwater in the gutters, and the fear that had gripped my neck relaxed its hold. My mother must have opened the door, gotten drenched, then come back inside. I knelt by her as she crouched next to the door, her hand on the knob, and said, "You're imagining things."

"I know what I saw." Brushing my hand off her shoulder, she stood up, anger illuminating her dark eyes. "He walked. He talked. He wanted to see you."

"Then where is he, Ma? I don't see anyone."

"Of course you don't." She sighed, as if I were the one unable to grasp the obvious. "He's a ghost, isn't he?"

Ever since my father died a few years ago, my mother and I lived together politely. We shared a passion for words, but I preferred the silence of writing while she loved to talk. She constantly fed me gossip and stories, the only kind I enjoyed concerning my father back when he was a man I did not know, young and happy. Then came stories of terror like the one about the reporter, the moral being that life, like the police, enjoys beating people now and again. Finally there was her favorite kind, the ghost story, of which she knew many, some firsthand.

"Aunt Six died of a heart attack at seventy-six," she told me once, twice, or perhaps three times, repetition being her habit. I never took her stories seriously. "She lived in Vung Tau and we were in Nha Trang. I was bringing dinner to the table when I saw Aunt Six sitting there in her nightgown. Her long gray hair, which she usually wore in a chignon, was loose and fell over her shoulders and in her face. I almost dropped the dishes. When I asked her what she was doing here, she just smiled. She stood up, kissed me, and turned me toward the kitchen. When I turned around again to see her, she was gone. It was her ghost. Uncle confirmed it when I called. She had passed away that morning, in her own bed."

Aunt Six died a good death, according to my mother, at home and with family, her ghost simply making the rounds to say farewell. My mother repeated her aunt's story while we sat at the kitchen table the morning she claimed to have seen my brother, her son. I had brewed her a pot of green tea and taken her temperature despite her protests, the result being, as she had predicted, normal. Waving the thermometer at me, she said he must have disappeared because he was tired. After all, he had just completed a journey of thousands of miles across the Pacific.

"So how did he get here?"

"He swam." She gave me a pitying look. "That's why he was wet."

"He was an excellent swimmer," I said, humoring her. "What did he look like?"

"Exactly the same."

"It's been twenty-five years. He hasn't changed at all?"

"They always look exactly the same as when you last saw them."

I remembered how he looked the last time, and any humor that I felt vanished. The stunned look on his face, the open eyes that did not flinch even with the splintered board of the boat's deck pressing against his cheek—I did not want to see him again, assuming there was something or someone to see. After my mother left for her shift at the salon, I tried to go back to sleep but could not. His eyes stared at me whenever I closed my own. Only now was I conscious of not having remembered him for months. I had long struggled to forget him, but just by turning a corner in the world or in my mind I could run into him, my best friend. From as far back as I can recall, I could hear his voice outside our house, calling my name. That was my signal to follow him down our village's lanes and pathways, through jackfruit and mango groves to the dikes and fields, dodging shattered palm trees and bomb craters. At the time, this was a normal childhood.

Looking back, however, I could see that we had passed our youth in a haunted country. Our father had been drafted, and we feared that he would never return. Before he left, he had dug a bomb shelter next to our home, a sandbagged bunker whose roof was braced by timber. Even though it was hot and airless, dank with the odor of the earth and alive with the movement of worms, we often went there to play as little children. When we were older, we went to study and tell stories. I was the best student in my school, excellent enough for my teacher to teach me English after hours, lessons I shared with my brother. He, in turn, told me tall tales, folklore, and rumors. When airplanes shrieked overhead and we huddled with my mother in the bunker, he whispered ghost stories into my ear to distract me. Except, he insisted, they were not ghost stories. They were historical accounts from reliable sources, the ancient crones who chewed betel nut and spat its red juice while squatting on their haunches in the market, tending coal stoves or overseeing baskets of wares. Our land's confirmed residents, they said, included the upper half of a Korean lieutenant, launched by a mine into the branches of a rubber tree; a scalped black American floating in the creek not far from his downed helicopter, his eyes and the exposed half-moon of his brain glistening above the water; and a decapitated Japanese private groping through cassava shrubbery for his head. These invaders came to conquer our land and now would never go home, the old ladies said, cackling and exposing lacquered teeth, or so my brother told me. I shivered with delight in the gloom, hearing those black-eyed women with my own ears, and it seemed to me that I would never tell stories like those.

Was it ironic, then, that I made a living from being a ghost-writer? I posed the question to myself as I lay in bed in the middle of the day, but the women with their black eyes and black teeth heard me. You call what you have a life? Their teeth clacked as they laughed at me. I pulled the covers up to

my nose, the way I used to do in my early years in America,
when creatures not only lurked in the hallway but also roamed
outside. My mother and father always peeked through the living room curtains before answering any knock, afraid of our
young countrymen, boys who had learned about violence from
growing up in wartime. "Don't open the door for someone
you don't know," my mother warned me, once, twice, three
times. "We don't want to end up like that family tied down
at gunpoint. They burned the baby with cigarettes until the
mother showed them where she hid her money." My American adolescence was filled with tales of woe like this, all of
them proof of what my mother said, that we did not belong
here. In a country where possessions counted for everything,
we had no belongings except our stories.

When knocking woke me, it was dark outside. My watch
said 6:35 in the evening. The knock came again, gentle, tentative. Despite myself, I knew who it was. I had locked the
bedroom door just in case, and now I pulled the covers over
my head, my heart beating fast. I willed him to go away, but
when he started rattling the doorknob, I knew I had no choice
but to rise. The fine hairs of my body stood at attention with
me as I watched the doorknob tremble with the pressure of
his grip. I reminded myself that he had given up his life for
me. The least I could do was open the door.

He was bloated and pale, hair feathery, skin dark, clad
in black shorts and a ragged gray T-shirt, arms and legs bony.
The last time I had seen him, he was taller by a head; now
our situations were reversed. When he said my name, his

voice was hoarse and raspy, not at all like his adolescent alto. His eyes, though, were the same, curious, as were his lips, slightly parted, always prepared to speak. A purple bruise with undertones of black gleamed on his left temple, but the blood I remembered was gone, washed away, I suppose, by salt water and storms. Even though it was not raining, he was water-soaked. I could smell the sea on him, and worse, I could smell the boat, rancid with human sweat and excreta.

When he said my name, I trembled, but this was a ghost of someone whom I loved and would never harm, the kind of ghost who, my mother had said, would not harm me. "Come in," I said, which seemed to me the bravest thing I could say. Unmoved, he looked at the carpet on which he was dripping water. When I brought him a clean T-shirt and shorts, along with a towel, he looked at me expectantly until I turned around and let him change. The clothes were my smallest but still a size too large for him, the shorts extending to his knees, the T-shirt voluminous. I motioned him in, and this time he obeyed, sitting on my rumpled bed. He refused to meet my gaze, seemingly more fearful of me than I was of him. While he was still fifteen I was thirty-eight, no longer an exuberant tomboy, reluctant to talk unless I had a purpose, as was the case when I interviewed Victor. Being an author, even one of the third or fourth rank, involved an etiquette I could live up to. But what does one say to a ghost, except to ask why he was here? I was afraid of the answer, so instead I said, "What took you so long?"

He looked at my bare toes with their bare nails. Perhaps he sensed that I was not good with children. Motherhood was too intimate for me, as were relationships lasting more than one night.

"You had to swim. It takes a long time to go so far, doesn't it?"

"Yes." His mouth remained open, as if he wanted to say more but was uncertain of what to say or how to say it. Perhaps this apparition was the first consequence of what my mother considered my unnatural nature, childless and single. Perhaps he was not a figment of my imagination but a symptom of something wrong, like the cancer that killed my father. His was also a good death, according to my mother, surrounded by family at home, not like what happened to her son and, nearly, to me. Panic surged from that bottomless well within myself that I had sealed with concrete, and I was relieved to hear the front door opening. "Mother will want to see you," I said. "Wait here. I'll be right back."

When we returned, we found only his wet clothes and the wet towel. She held up the gray T-shirt, the same as he had worn on the blue boat with the red eyes.

"Now you know," my mother said. "Never turn your back on a ghost."

The black shorts and gray T-shirt stank of brine and were heavy with more than just water. When I carried them to the kitchen, the weight of the clothes in my hands was the weight of evidence. I had seen him wear these clothes on dozens of occasions. I remembered them when the shorts were not black with grime but still pristine blue, when the shirt was not gray and ragged but white and neat. "Do you believe now?" my mother said, lifting the lid of the washing machine. I hesitated. Some people say that faith burns inside them, but my newfound faith was chilling to me. "Yes," I said. "I believe."

The machine hummed in the background as we sat for dinner at the kitchen table, the air anointed with star anise and ginger. "That's how come it took him so many years," my mother said, blowing onto her hot soup. Nothing had ever daunted her appetite or dented her cast-iron stomach, not even the events on the boat or the apparition of her son. "He swam the entire distance."

"Aunt Six lived hundreds of miles away and you saw her the same day."

"Ghosts don't live by our rules. Each ghost is different. Good ghosts, bad ghosts, happy ghosts, sad ghosts. Ghosts of people who die when they're old, when they're young, when they're small. You think baby ghosts behave the same as grandfather ghosts?"

I knew nothing about ghosts. I had not believed in ghosts and neither did anyone else I knew except for my mother and Victor, who himself seemed spectral, the heat of grief rendering him pale and nearly translucent, his only color coming from a burst of uncombed red hair. Even with him the otherworldly came up only twice, once on the phone and once in his living room. Nothing had been touched since the day his family left for the airport, not even the sorrowful dust.

I had the impression that the windows had not been opened since that day, as if he wanted to preserve the depleted air that his wife and children had breathed before they suffered their bad deaths, so far from home. "The dead move on," he had said, coiled in his armchair, hands between his thighs. "But the living, we just stay here."

These words opened his last chapter, the one I worked on after my mother went to sleep and I descended into the bright basement, illuminated with fluorescent tubes. I wrote one sentence, then paused to listen for a knock or steps on the stairway. My rhythm through the night was established, a few lines followed by a wait for something that did not come, the next day more of the same. The conclusion of Victor's memoir was in sight when my mother came home from the nail salon with shopping bags from Chinatown, one full of groceries, the other with underwear, a pair of pajamas, blue jeans, a denim jacket, a pack of socks, knit gloves, a baseball cap. After stacking them next to his dried and ironed T-shirt and shorts, she said, "He can't be wandering out in the cold with what you gave him, like a homeless person or some il-legal immigrant." When I said that I hadn't thought of it that way, she snorted, annoyed by my ignorance of the needs of ghosts. Only after dinner did she warm up again. Her mood had improved because instead of retreating to my basement as usual, I had stayed to watch one of the soap operas she rented by the armfuls, serials of beautiful Korean people snared in romantic tangles. "If we hadn't had a war," she said that night, her wistfulness drawing me closer, "we'd be like the Koreans

now. Saigon would be Seoul, your father alive, you married
with children, me a retired housewife, not a manicurist." Her
hair was in curlers, and a bowl of watermelon seeds was in
her lap. "I'd spend my days visiting friends and being visited,
and when I died, a hundred people would come to my funeral.
I'd be lucky if twenty people will come here, with you taking
care of things. That frightens me more than anything. You
can't even remember to take out the garbage or pay the bills.
You won't even go outside to shop for groceries."

"I'd remember to take care of your soul."

"When would you hold the wake? When would the cele-
bration of my death anniversary be? What would you say?"

"Write it down for me," I said. "What I'm supposed to
say."

"Your brother would have known what to do," she said.
"That's what sons are for."

To this I had no reply.

When he had still not appeared by eleven, my mother went
to sleep. I descended to my basement once more and tried to
write. Writing was entering into fog, feeling my way for a route
from this world to the unearthly world of words, a route easier
to find on some days than others. Lurking on my shoulder
as I stumbled through the grayness was the parrot of a question, asking me how I lived and he died. I was younger and
weaker, yet it was my brother we buried, letting him slip into
the ocean without a shroud or a word from me. The wailing of

my mother and the sobbing of my father rose in my memory, but neither drowned out my own silence. Now it was right to say a few words, to call him back as he must have wanted, but I could not find them. Just when I thought another night would pass without his return, I heard the knock at the top of the stairs. I believe, I reminded myself. I believe that he would never harm me.

"Don't knock," I said when I opened the door. "It's your home, too."

He merely stared at me, and we lapsed into an awkward silence. Then he said, "Thank you." His voice was stronger now, almost as high-pitched as I remembered, and this time he did not look away. He still wore my T-shirt and shorts, but when I showed him the clothes that my mother had bought, he said, "I don't need those."

"You're wearing what I gave you."

His silence went on for so long I thought he might not have heard me.

"We wear them for the living," he said at last. "Not for us."

I led him to the couch. "You mean ghosts?"

He sat down next to me, considering my question before answering.

"We always knew ghosts existed," he said.

"I had my doubts." I held his hand. "Why have you come back?"

His gaze was discomforting. He had not blinked once.

"I haven't come back," he said. "I've come here."

"You haven't left this world yet?"

He nodded.

"Why not?"

Again he was silent. Finally he said, "Why do you think?"

I looked away. "I've tried to forget."

"But you haven't."

"I can't."

I had not forgotten our nameless blue boat and it had not forgotten me, the red eyes painted on either side of its prow having never ceased to stare me down. After four uneventful days on a calm sea under blue skies and clear nights, islands at last came into view, black stitching on the faraway horizon. It was then that another ship appeared in the distance, aiming for us. It was swift and we were slow, burdened with more than a hundred people in a fishing boat meant to hold only a fishing boat's crew and a fishing boat's load of cold mackerel. My brother took me into the cramped engine room with its wheezing motor and used his pocketknife to slash my long hair into the short, jagged boy's cut I still wore. "Don't speak," he said. He was fifteen and I was thirteen. "You still sound like a girl. Now take off your shirt."

I always did as he told me, in this case shyly, even though he hardly glanced at me as he ripped my shirt into strips. He bound my barely noticeable breasts with the fabric, then took off his own shirt and buttoned me into it, leaving himself with just his ragged T-shirt. Then he smeared engine oil on my face and we huddled in the dark until the pirates came for us. These fishermen resembled our fathers and brothers, sinewy and brown, except that they wielded machetes and machine guns. We turned over our gold, watches, earrings, wedding bands, and jade. Then they seized the teenage girls and young women, a dozen of them, shooting a father and a husband who had protested. Everyone fell silent except those being dragged away, screaming and crying. I didn't know any of them, girls from other villages, and this made it easier for me to pray I would not be one of them as I pressed against my brother's arm. Only when the last of the girls had been thrown onto the deck of the pirate ship, the pirates climbing back on board after them, did I breathe again.

The last man to leave glanced at me in passing. He was my father's age, his nose a sunburned pig's foot, his odor a mix of sweat and the viscera of fish. This little man, who spoke some of our language, stepped close and lifted my chin. "You're a handsome boy," he said. After my brother stabbed him with his pocketknife, the three of us stood there in astonishment, our gaze on the blade, tipped by blood, a silent moment broken when the little man howled in pain, drew back his machine gun, and swung its stock hard against my brother's head. The crack—I could hear it still. He fell with the force of dead weight, blood streaming from his brow, jaw and temple hitting the wooden deck with an awful thud still resonant in my memory.

I touched the bruise. "Does it hurt?"

"Not any more. Does it still hurt for you?"

Once more I pretended to think about a question whose answer I already knew. "Yes," I said at last. When the little man threw me to the deck, the fall bruised the back of my head.

When he ripped my shirt off, he drew blood with his sharp fingernails. When I turned my face away and saw my mother and father screaming, my eardrums seemed to have burst, for I could hear nothing. Even when I screamed I could not hear myself, even though I felt my mouth opening and closing. The world was muzzled, the way it would be ever afterward with my mother and father and myself, none of us uttering another sound on this matter. Their silence and my own would cut me again and again. But what pained me the most was not any of these things, nor the weight of the men on me. It was the light shining into my dark eyes as I looked to the sky and saw the smoldering tip of God's cigarette, poised in the heavens the moment before it was pressed against my skin.

Since then I avoid day and sun. Even he noticed, holding up his forearm against mine to show me I was whiter than he was. We had done the same in the bunker, splaying our hands in front of our faces to see if they were visible in the dark. We wanted to know we were still all there, coated in the dust that sifted onto us after each impact, the memory of the American jets screaming overhead making me tremble. The first time we heard them, he whispered in my ear not to worry. They were only Phantoms.

"Do you know what I liked the most about those times?" He shook his head. We sat on the sofa of my basement office, warmer than the living room in November. "We would come outside after the bombing, you holding my hand while we stood blinking in the sun. What I loved was how after the darkness of hiding there came the light. And after all that thunder, silence."

He nodded, unblinking, curled up on the sofa like me, our knees touching. The parrot crouched on my shoulder, roosting there ever since we let my brother go into the sea, and it came to me that letting it speak was the only way to get rid of it.

"Tell me something," it said. "Why did I live and you die?"

He regarded me with eyes that would not dry out no matter how long they stayed open. Mother was wrong. He had changed, the proof being those eyes, preserved in brine for so long they would remain forever open.

"You died too," he said. "You just don't know it."

I remembered a conversation with Victor. A question struck me one night at eleven, so urgent that I telephoned him, knowing he'd be awake. "Yes, I believe in ghosts," he said, not surprised to hear from me. I could see him curled up on his chair, head aflame on his candle-wax body, as if he were lit up by the memory of the airplane crash that had taken the lives of his family. When I asked him if he had ever seen any ghosts, he said, "All the time. When I close my eyes, my wife and children appear just like when they were alive. With my eyes open, I'll see them in my peripheral vision. They move fast and disappear before I can focus on them. But I smell them too, my wife's perfume when she walks by, the shampoo in my daughter's hair, the sweat in my son's jerseys. And I can feel them, my son brushing his hand on mine, my wife breathing on my neck the way she used to do in bed, my daughter clinging to my knees. And last of all, you hear ghosts. My wife tells me to check for my keys before I leave the house. My daughter reminds me not to burn the toast. My son asks me to rake the leaves so he can jump in them. They all sing happy birthday to me."

Victor's birthday had been two weeks ago, and what it was that I imagined—him sitting in the dark, eyes closed, listening for echoes of birthdays past—became the opening of his memoir.

"Aren't you afraid of ghosts?" I asked.

Over the line, in the silence, the static hissed.

"You aren't afraid of the things you believe in," he said.

This, too, I wrote in his memoir, even though I had not understood what he meant.

Now I did. My body clenched as I sobbed without shame and without fear. My brother watched me curiously as I wept for him and for me, for all the years we could have had together but didn't, for all the words never spoken between my mother, my father, and me. Most of all, I cried for those other girls who had vanished and never come back, including myself.

When it was published a few months later, Victor's memoir sold well. The critics had kind things to say. My name was nowhere to be found in it, but my small reputation grew a little larger among those who worked in the shadows of publishing. My agent called to offer me another memoir on even more lucrative terms, the story of a soldier who lost his arms and legs trying to defuse a bomb. I declined. I was writing a book of my own.

"Ghost stories?" Her tone was approving. "I can sell that. People love being frightened."

I did not tell her that I had no desire to terrify the living. Not all ghosts were bent on vengeance and mayhem. My ghosts were the quiet and shy ones like my brother, as well as the mournful revenants in my mother's stories. It was my mother, the expert on ghosts, who told me my brother was not going to return. He had disappeared when I turned my back on him, reaching for a box of tissues. There was only a depression in the sofa where he had sat, cold to the touch. I went upstairs to wake her, and after putting the teakettle on the stove, she sat down with me at the kitchen table to hear of her son's visit. Having cried over him for years, she did not cry now.

"You know he's gone for good, don't you? He came and said all he wanted to say."

The teakettle began rattling and blowing steam through its one nostril.

"Ma," I said. "I haven't said all I wanted to say."

And my mother, who had not looked away from me on the deck of the boat, looked away now. For all the ghost stories she possessed, there was one story she did not want to tell, one type of company she did not want to keep. They were there in the kitchen with us, the ghosts of the refugees and the ghosts of the pirates, the ghost of the boat watching us with those eyes that never closed, even the ghost of the girl I once was, the only ghosts my mother feared.

"Tell me a story, Ma," I said. "I'm listening."

She found one easily, as I knew she would. "There was once a woman," she said, "deeply in love with her husband, a soldier who disappears on a mission behind enemy lines. He is reported dead; she refuses to believe it. The war ends and she flees to this new country, eventually marrying again decades later. She is happy until the day her first husband returns from the dead, released from the camp where he has suffered as a secret prisoner for nearly thirty years." As proof, my mother showed me a newspaper clipping with a photograph of the woman and her first husband, reunited at the airport some years ago. Their gazes do not meet. They look shy, uncomfortable, forlorn, surrounded by friends and reporters who cannot see the two ghosts also present at this melancholic meeting, the smudged shadows of their former selves.

"These kinds of stories happen all the time," my mother said, pouring me a cup of green tea. This evening séance would be our new nightly ritual, my mother an old lady, myself an aging one. "Why write down what I'm telling you?"

"Someone has to," I said, notepad on my lap, pen at attention.

"Writers." She shook her head, but I think she was pleased. "At least you won't just be making things up like you usually do."

Sometimes this is how stories come to me, through her. "Let me tell you a story," she would say, once, twice, or perhaps three times. More often, though, I go hunting for the ghosts, something I can do without ever leaving home. As they haunt our country, so do we haunt theirs. They are pallid creatures, more frightened of us than we are of them. That is why we see these shades so rarely, and why we must seek them out. The talismans on my desk, a tattered pair of shorts and a ragged T-shirt, clean and dry, neatly pressed, remind me that my mother was right. Stories are just things we fabricate, nothing more. We search for them in a world besides our own, then leave them here to be found, garments shed by ghosts.

THE OTHER MAN

*L*iem's plan was to walk calmly past the waiting crowd after he disembarked, but instead he found himself hesitating at the gate, anxiously scanning the strange faces. In one hand he held his duffel bag, and in the other he clutched the form given to him by Mrs. Lindemulder, the woman with the horn-rimmed glasses from the refugee service. When she had seen him off at the San Diego airport, she'd told him his sponsor, Parrish Coyne, would be waiting in San Francisco. The flight was only his second trip by air, and he'd passed it crumpling and uncrumpling an empty pretzel bag, until his seatmate asked him if he would please stop. American etiquette confused him, for Americans could sometimes be very polite, and at other times rather rude, jostling by him as they did now in their rush to disembark. The lingering pressure in his ears bewildered him further, making it hard for him to understand the PA system's distorted English. He was wondering if he was missing something important when he spotted the man who must be Parrish Coyne, standing near the back of the crowd and holding up a hand-lettered placard with MR. LIEM printed neatly on it in red. The sight nearly overwhelmed Liem with relief and gratitude, for no one had ever called him "mister" before.

Parrish Coyne was middle-aged and, except for his gray ponytail, distinguished-looking, his deep-set green eyes resting above a thin, straight nose. He wore a brown fedora and a black leather jacket, unbuttoned over a generous belly. After Liem shyly approached him, but before Liem could say a word, he said Liem's name twice. "Li-am, I presume?" Parrish spoke with an English accent as he clasped Liem's hand and mispronounced his name, using two syllables instead of one. "Li-am, is it?"

"Yes," Liem said, guessing that his foreignness was evident to all. "That is me." He meant to correct Parrish's pronunciation, but before he could do so, Parrish unexpectedly hugged him, leaving him to pat the man's shoulder awkwardly, aware of other people watching them and wondering, no doubt, about their relationship. Then Parrish stepped back and gripped his shoulders, staring at him with an intensity that made Liem self-conscious, unused as he was to being the object of such scrutiny.

"To be honest," Parrish announced at last, "I didn't expect you to be so pretty."

"Really?" Liem kept smiling and said no more. He wasn't sure he'd heard right, but he'd learned to bide his time in situations like this, sticking to monosyllables until the course of a conversation clarified matters.

"Stop it," the young man next to Parrish said, also with an English accent. "You're embarrassing him." Just then the pressure in Liem's eardrums popped, and the muffled sounds of the terminal swelled to a normal volume and clarity.

"This is Marcus Chan," Parrish said, "my good friend."

Marcus appeared to be in his mid-twenties, only a few years older than Liem, who'd turned eighteen over the summer. If Marcus's smile seemed a little disdainful as he offered his hand, Liem could hardly blame him, for compared with Marcus, he was sorely lacking in just about every regard. Even the yellowness of his teeth was more evident next to the whiteness of Marcus's. With body erect and head tilted back, Marcus had the posture of someone expecting an inheritance, while Liem's sense of debt caused him to walk with eyes downcast, as if searching for pennies. Since he was shorter than both Marcus and Parrish, he was forced to look up as he said, "I am very happy to meet you." Out of sheer nervousness, Marcus's hand still gripped in his, he added, "San Francisco number one."

"That's lovely." Marcus gently let go of his hand. "What's number two then?"

"Hush." Parrish frowned. "Why not be helpful and take Liem's bag?"

With Marcus carrying the duffel bag and trailing behind, Parrish guided Liem through the terminal, hand on elbow. "It must seem very overwhelming to you," Parrish said, waving in a way that took in the crowds, the terminal, and presumably all of San Francisco. "I can only imagine how strange this all appears. Coming here from England was enough of a culture shock for me."

Liem glanced over his shoulder at Marcus. "You come from England, too?"

"Hong Kong," Marcus said. "You could say I'm an honorary Englishman."

"In any case," Parrish said, squeezing Liem's elbow and bending his head to speak more confidentially into Liem's ear, "you must have had an awful time of it."

"No, not very bad." Liem spoke with nonchalance, even though the prospect of rehearsing his story one more time flooded him with dread. In the four months since he'd fled Saigon, he'd been asked for his story again and again, by sailors, marines, and social workers, their questions becoming all too predictable. What was it like? How do you feel? Isn't it all so *sad?* Sometimes he told the curious that what had happened was a long story, which only impelled them to ask for a shorter version. It was this edited account that he offered as Marcus drove the car through the parking garage, into the streets, and onto the freeway. Casting himself as just one more anonymous young refugee, he recounted a drama that began with leaving his parents in Long Xuyen last summer, continued with his work in a so-called tea bar in Saigon, and climaxed with the end of the war. Even this brief version tired him, and as he spoke he leaned his forehead against the window, watching the orderly traffic on the wide highway.

"So," he said. "Now I am here."

Parrish sighed from the front seat of the sedan. "That war wasn't just a tragedy," he said, "but a farce." Marcus made a noise in his throat that might have been an assent before he turned up the volume on the radio a few notches. A woman was uttering an encomium to a brand of furniture polish, something to bring out the luster without using a duster. "You'll find the weather here to be cold and gray, even though it's September," Marcus said. "In the winter it will rain. Not exactly the monsoon, but you'll get used to it." As he drove, he pointed to passing landmarks, the standouts in Liem's memory being Candlestick Park with its formidable walls, and the choppy, marbled waters of the bay. Then, as traffic from another freeway merged with theirs and the car slowed down, Parrish lowered the volume on the radio and said, "There's something you need to know about Marcus and myself."

A white passenger van, accelerating on the right, blocked Liem's view of the bay. He turned from the window to meet Parrish's gaze. "Yes?"

"We're a couple," Parrish announced. Out of the corner of his eye, Liem saw the white van edging forward, past the shrinking blot of moisture left by his forehead on the window. "In the romantic sense," Parrish added. Liem decided that "in the romantic sense" must be an idiomatic expression, the kind Mrs. Lindemulder had said Americans used often, like "you're killing me" and "he drives me up the wall." In idiomatic English, a male couple in the romantic sense must simply mean very close friends, and he smiled politely until he saw Marcus staring at him in the rearview mirror, the gaze sending a nervous tremor through his gut.

"Okay," Liem said. "Wow."

"I hope you're not too shocked."

"No, no." The small hairs on his arms and on the back of his neck stiffened as they'd done before whenever another boy, deliberately or by chance, had brushed his elbow, sometimes his knee, while they walked hand-in-hand or sat on park benches with their arms slung over each other's shoulders, watching traffic and girls pass by. "I am liberal."

"Then I hope you'll stay with us."

"And open-minded," he added. In truth he had no other refuge but Parrish's hospitality, just as there was nowhere else for him to go at the end of the day in Saigon but a crowded room of single men and boys, restless on reed mats as they tried to sleep while breathing air humidified with the odor of bodies worked hard. "Do not worry."

"Good," Marcus said, turning the volume up again, the way one of the boys would around midnight, on his transistor radio, when everyone knew but wouldn't say that sleep was impossible. Liem's eyes were closed by then, but he couldn't help seeing the faces of men he knew casually or had watched in the tea bar, even those of his own roommates. In the darkness, he heard the rustle of mosquito netting as the others masturbated also. The next morning, everyone looked at each other blankly, and nobody spoke of what had occurred the previous evening, as if it were an atrocity in the jungle better left buried.

He thought he'd forgotten about those nights, had run away from them at last, but now he wondered if the evidence still existed in the lines of his palms. He rubbed his hands uneasily on his jeans as they drove through a neighborhood with bustling sidewalks, trafficked by people of several colors. They were mostly whites and Mexicans, along with some blacks and a scattering of Chinese, none of whom looked twice at the signs in the store windows or the graffiti on the walls, written in a language he'd never seen before: PELUQUERÍA, CHUY ES MARICÓN, RITMO LATINO, DENTISTA, IGLESIA DE CRISTO, VIVA LA RAZA!

After turning onto a street lined with parked cars jammed fender-to-fender, Marcus swung the sedan nose-down into the sloping driveway of a narrow two-story house, upon whose scarlet door was hung, strangely enough, a portrait of the Virgin Mary. "We're home," Parrish said. Later Liem would learn that Parrish was an ambivalent Catholic, that the district they lived in was the Mission, and that the name for the house's architectural style was Victorian, but today all he noticed was its color.

"Purple?" he said, never having seen a home painted in this fashion before.

Parrish chuckled and opened his door. "Close," he said. "It's mauve."

* * *

Mrs. Lindemulder had squeezed Liem's shoulder in the San Diego airport and warned him that in San Francisco the people tended to be unique, an implication he hadn't understood at the time. Every day for the first few weeks in Parrish's house, Liem wanted to phone Mrs. Lindemulder and tell her she'd made a huge mistake, but Parrish's generosity shamed him and prevented him from doing so. Instead, he stood in front of the mirror each morning and told himself there was nobody to fear, except himself. He'd silently said the same thing last year, at summer's end in '74, when he bade farewell to his parents at the bus station in Long Xuyen. He hadn't complained about being dispatched alone to Saigon, several hours north, where he'd be the family's lifeline. As the eldest son, he had duties, and he was used to working, having done so since leaving school at the age of twelve to shine the boots of American soldiers.

He'd known them since he was eight, when he began picking through their garbage dumps for tin and cardboard, well-worn *Playboy* magazines, and unopened C rations. The GIs taught him the rudiments of English, enough for him to find a job years later in Saigon, sweeping the floor of a tea bar on Tu Do Street where the girls pawned themselves for dollars. With persistence, he sandpapered the two discourses of junkyard and whorehouse into a more usable kind of English, good enough to let him understand the rumor passed from one foreign journalist to another in the spring of '75, six months ago. Thousands would be slaughtered if the city fell to the Communists.

In April, when rockets and mortars began exploding on the outskirts of the city, the rumor seemed about to come true. Although he hadn't planned on kicking, shoving, and clawing his way aboard a river barge, he found himself doing so one morning after he saw a black cloud of smoke over the airport, burning on the horizon, lit up by enemy shellfire. A month later he was in Camp Pendleton, San Diego, waiting for sponsorship. He and the other refugees had been rescued by a Seventh Fleet destroyer in the South China Sea, taken to a makeshift Marine Corps camp at Guam, and then flown to California. As he lay on his cot and listened to children playing hide-and-seek in the alleys between the tents, he tried to forget the people who had clutched at the air as they fell into the river, some knocked down in the scramble, others shot in the back by desperate soldiers clearing a way for their own escape. He tried to forget what he'd discovered, how little other lives mattered to him when his own was at stake.

None of this was mentioned in the airmail he posted to his parents, soon after coming to Parrish's house. It was his second letter home. In June, at Camp Pendleton, he'd dispatched his first airmail care of the resettlement agency. In both cases, assuming no letter would go unread by the Communists, he wrote only of where he lived and how to get in touch with him. He was afraid of endangering his family by marking them as relatives of someone who'd fled, and he was even more afraid the letters might never make it home at all. The only time his family's fate wasn't on his mind was during those few seconds after he woke up, in a warm bed under three blankets, remembering dreams in which he spoke perfect English. Then he opened his eyes to see a faint blue glow filtered through foggy windows, the murky and wavering shimmer reminding him of where he was, in a distant city, a foreign place where even the quality of light differed from the tropical glare he'd always known.

Downstairs, he would find Parrish and Marcus eating breakfast and discussing the local news, international politics, or the latest film. They bickered often, usually in a bantering way, about whether or not they should vote for Jimmy Carter or Gerald Ford, or whether Ford's would-be assassin, a San Francisco woman, should get life or death.

When they began arguing seriously in front of him, he knew he was becoming a part of their household. Sometimes the fights seemed to occur for no reason, as happened one morning in October after Parrish asked about the date of Marcus's final exams. "Why don't you take them for me?" Marcus snapped before stalking out of the kitchen. Parrish waited until Marcus ran up the stairs before he leaned over to Liem and said, "It's the terrible twos. The second year's the hardest."

"Oh, yes?" Liem nodded his head even though he was uncertain, once again, about what Parrish meant. "I see you both yell many times."

"Even though he's older, he's not as mature as you," Parrish said. He stirred his coffee, his spoon making figure eights instead of circles. "He hasn't seen the things you or I have. Of course, when I was his age, I was spoiled and a little lazy too. But I'm better now. My ancestors made their money from means of which I'm ashamed, but there's no reason why I can't put my own to some good use. Is there?"

"No?"

"No," Parrish said. Liem understood he was one of the good uses for the money Parrish had earned in two decades as a corporate accountant, a job he'd given up a few years before to work in environmental protection. Although Parrish refused to let Liem pay rent, Liem had found a job anyway. The week after his arrival, he'd wandered through downtown until he came across a liquor store in the heart of the Tenderloin, on the corner of Taylor and Turk. "Help Wanted" was scrawled in soap on the window next to "Se Habla Español." The book he carried in his pocket, *Everyday Dialogues in English*, had no scenarios featuring the duo patrolling the corner outside the store, so he said nothing as he brushed by the shivering prostitute with pimples in her cleavage, who dismissed him at a look, and the transvestite with hairy forearms, who did not.

His shift ran from eight in the morning to eight in the evening, six days a week, his day off on Thursday. He swept the floor and stocked the shelves, cleaned the toilet and wiped the windows, tended the register and then repeated the routine. During downtime, he read his book, hoping for clues on how to talk with Marcus and Parrish, but finding little of use in chapters like "Juan Gonzalez Visits New York City and Has to Ask His Way Around," or "An Englishman and an American Attend a Football Game." At the end of his shift, he dragged two garbage bags to a Dumpster down an alley where people with questionable histories urinated and vomited when it was dark, and sometimes when it wasn't. No matter how much he scrubbed his hands afterward, he sensed they'd never really be clean. The grease and garbage he dealt in had worked their way into his calluses so deeply he imagined that he was forever leaving his fingerprints everywhere.

By the time he returned to the Victorian, Parrish and Marcus had already finished dinner, and he ate leftovers in the kitchen while they watched television. As soon as he was done, he retreated upstairs, where he showered off the day's sweat and tried not to think of Marcus's lean, pale body. The endless hot water left him pliant and calm, and it was in this relaxed state of mind that he opened the door of the bathroom one evening after his shower, wrapped only in a towel, to encounter Marcus padding down the hallway. They faced each other in silence before both stepped to the same side. Then they both stepped to the other side, feet shuffling so awkwardly that the laugh track from the sitcom Parrish was watching downstairs, audible even on the landing, seemed to be directed at them.

"Excuse me," Liem said finally, his back slick with sweat from the heat of the long shower. "May I pass?"

Marcus shrugged, his eyes flickering once over Liem's body before he bowed slightly, in a mocking fashion, and said, "Yes, you may."

Liem hurried past Marcus and into his room. As soon as he shut the door, he leaned against it, ear pressed to wood, but another burst of canned laughter from downstairs made it impossible to hear Marcus's footsteps fading down the hallway.

On an overcast Thursday morning in mid-November, Marcus and Liem drove Parrish to the airport. He was spending the weekend in Washington, at a conference on nuclear power's threat to the environment. As the wind beat against the windows, Parrish explained how the government buried its spent plutonium and uranium in the desert, where they poisoned land and threatened lives for millennia. "And mostly poor lives at that," Parrish said. "Just think of it as a gigantic minefield in our backyard." Marcus drummed his fingers on the steering wheel as he drove, but Parrish gave no sign of noticing. On the curb at the airport, his suitcase at his feet, he kissed Marcus good-bye and hugged Liem. "See you Sunday night," Parrish said before shutting the passenger door behind Liem. Liem was waving through the window, and Parrish was waving back, when Marcus accelerated into traffic without so much as a glance over his shoulder.

"When's he going to stop trying to save the world?" Marcus demanded. "It's getting to be a bore."

Liem buckled his seat belt. "But Parrish is a good person."

"There's a reason why saints are martyred. Nobody can stand them."

They rode in silence for the next quarter of an hour, until they neared the center of the city. There, the sight of a bakery truck entering the freeway from Army Street made Liem ask, "Are you hungry? I am hungry."

"Don't say I *am* hungry, say *I'm* hungry. You have to learn how to use contractions if you want to speak like a native."

"I'm hungry. Are you?"

The restaurant Marcus chose in Chinatown was on Jackson Street and nearly the size of a ballroom, with pillars of dark cherrywood and tasseled red lanterns hanging from the ceiling. Even on a Thursday morning it was noisy and bustling; waitresses in smocks pushed carts up and down the aisles while bow-tied waiters hurried from table to table, checks and pots of tea in hand. They sat by a window overlooking Jackson Street, the sight of Asian crowds comforting to Liem. As the train of carts rolled by, Marcus picked and rejected expertly from the offerings, ordering in Cantonese and explaining in English as the varieties of dim sum were heaped before them in a daunting display, including shiu mai, dumplings of minced pork and scallions, long-stemmed Chinese broccoli, and sliced roasted pork with candied skin the color of watermelon seeds. "Parrish won't touch those," Marcus said approvingly as he watched Liem suck the dimpled skin off a chicken's foot, leaving only the twiggy bones.

After the waiter swept away the dishes, they sat quietly with a tin pot of chrysanthemum tea between them. Liem rolled the bottom of his teacup in a circle around a grease stain on the tablecloth before he asked Marcus about his family, something Marcus had never discussed in front of him.

All Liem knew about Marcus was that he'd lived in Hong Kong until he was eighteen, that he was enrolled in business administration at San Francisco State but hardly ever went there, and that he worked out at the gym every day. His father, Marcus said with a snort, was an executive at a rubber company who had sent him to study overseas, expecting he would eventually return to help run the business. But three years ago a spiteful ex-lover had mailed his father one of Marcus's love letters, with candid pictures tucked into the folds. "Very candid pictures," Marcus said darkly. After that, his father had disowned him, and now Parrish paid his expenses. "Can you imagine anything worse?" Marcus concluded.

Liem wasn't sure whether Marcus was referring to the lover's betrayal, the father's plans, or Parrish's money. What he really wanted to know was what "candid" meant, but when Marcus only sipped his tea, not seeming to expect an answer, Liem spoke instead about his own family, all farmers, hawkers, and draftees. Nobody had ever traveled very far from Long Xuyen, unless he was drafted by the army. Liem was the family's first explorer, and perhaps that was the reason his parents were so anxious at the bus station in Long Xuyen, one of the few moments of his past he recalled with any clarity. The patch of unshaded dirt and cement was crowded with passengers ready to board, holding cartons tied with twine and keeping close watch on their pigs and chickens, shuffling in wire cages. As the heat rose in waves, the odor of human sweat and animal dung, thickened by the dust, rose with it.

"We raised you well," his father said, unable to look him in the eye with his own bluish-gray ones, hazy from cataracts. "I know you won't lose yourself in the city."

"I won't," Liem promised. "You can depend on me." He heard the driver shouting for passengers to board as his mother ran her hands up and down his arms and patted his chest, as if frisking him, before she squeezed a small wad of bills into his pocket. "Take care of yourself," she said. Around her mouth, deep wrinkles appeared to be stitches sewing her lips together. "I won't be able to anymore." He hadn't said he loved her, or his father, before he left. He'd been too distracted by his desperation to get on the bus, for without a seat he'd have to stand shoulder-to-shoulder in the aisle, or else risk his life riding on the roof all the way to Saigon.

"How could you know what was going to happen?" Marcus leaned forward. "You're not a fortune-teller. Anyway, that's all in the past. You can't dwell on it. The best way to help them now is to help yourself."

"Yeah," he said, even though this was, to him, a very American way of thinking.

"The point is, what do you want to be?"

"To be?"

"In the future. What do you want to do with yourself?"

No one had ever asked Liem such a question, and Liem rarely asked it of himself. He was content with his job at the liquor store, especially when he compared his fate with that of his friends back home. The underage ones, like him, had become bar sweeps or houseboys for Americans, while the older, luckier ones dodged army service, becoming thieves or pimps or rich men's servants. Unlucky ones got drafted, and very unlucky ones did not come home at all, or if they did, returned as beggars who laid their stumps on the side of the road.

Marcus was watching him expectantly. The idea of saying he wanted to be a doctor or a lawyer or a policeman was utterly ludicrous, but the desire to appear noble in Marcus's eyes, and maybe his own, seized him.

"I want to be good," he said at last.

"Well." Marcus glanced at the bill. "Don't we all."

The next day at the liquor store, Liem counted seconds by sweeps of his broom and rings of the register, his shift threatening never to end when only yesterday he'd hoped the day would run on forever. After he'd grabbed the check from Marcus and paid for the dim sum, they had browsed the curio shops of Chinatown together, then driven to Treasure Island to see the Golden Gate Bridge, winding up by dusk in a Market Street theater, where they sat knee-to-knee watching *One Flew over the Cuckoo's Nest*. Later, eating sushi at a Japanese restaurant on Sutter in Japantown, neither mentioned the contact—they talked instead about Jack Nicholson, whose films Liem had never seen; and Western Europe, which Liem had never visited; and the varieties of sushi, which Liem had never eaten before. In short, Marcus did most of the talking, and that was fine with Liem.

Talking with Marcus was easy, because all Liem had to do was ask questions. Marcus, however, rarely asked him anything, and during those moments when Liem ran out of inquiries, silence ensued, and the hum of the car or the chatter of the other diners became uncomfortably noticeable. Neither spoke of Parrish, not even when they returned to the Victorian and Marcus opened one of Parrish's bottles of red wine, a Napa Valley pinot noir. Never having drunk wine before, Liem woke up the next morning feeling as if the corkscrew had been driven into his forehead. He could barely crawl out of bed and to the bathroom, where, as he brushed his teeth, he vaguely remembered Marcus helping him up the stairs and easing him into bed. Seeing no sign of him before he went to work, he concluded Marcus was sleeping in.

When he returned to the Victorian in the evening, he found Marcus watching television in the living room, clad in his bathrobe and with his hair mussed. "A letter came for you today," Marcus said, switching off the television with the remote control. On the coffee table was a battered blue airmail marked by an unmistakable handwriting, the pen marks so forceful they almost cut through the thin envelope. Liem's father had replied to his first note, the airmail addressed to him at Camp Pendleton and forwarded by the resettlement agency in San Diego.

"Aren't you going to open it?" Marcus said.

"No," he muttered. "I don't think so." He rubbed the envelope between his fingers, unable to explain how he'd dreaded the letter's arrival as much as he'd yearned for it.

Once he opened the letter, his life would change again, and perhaps he wanted it to stay the same. Summoning all his will, he laid the airmail on the coffee table again and sat down next to Marcus on the couch, where together they stared at the blue envelope as if it were an anonymous letter slipped under an adulterer's door.

"They think we've got a Western disease," Marcus said. "Or so my father says."

"We?" Liem said.

"Don't think I don't know."

Liem kept his eyes on the letter, certain his father had written no more than what needed to be said: *make money and send it home, take care and be good.* The message would be underlined once and then once more, leaving him to guess at anything too dangerous to be said in his father's bare vocabulary. But whereas his father had never sought to find new words, Liem was the opposite. He looked up at Marcus and asked the question he'd wanted to ask since yesterday.

"What does candid mean?"

"Candid?" Marcus said. "Yeah, right. Candid. It means being caught by surprise, like in a photograph or a film, when someone takes your picture and you're not looking. Or it means someone who's frank. Who's honest and direct."

Liem took a deep breath. "I want to be candid."

"I'd like to be candid."

"Shut up," Liem said, putting his hand on Marcus's knee.

* * *

Afterward, he sensed things might not have gone well. First, none of their clothes came off as smoothly as he expected, because all of a sudden the buttons and zippers were smaller than he knew them to be, and his fingers larger and clumsier. His rhythm seemed to be off, too. Sometimes in his eagerness he moved too fast, and to make up for it, or because he was embarrassed, he then went too slowly, throwing them out of sync and causing him to apologize repeatedly for an elbow here, or a knee there, until Marcus said, "Stop saying you're sorry and just enjoy yourself, for heaven's sake." So he did his best to relax and give himself up to the experience. Later, his arm thrown over Marcus's body, facing his back, Liem wasn't surprised to discover how little he remembered. His habit of forgetting was too deeply ingrained, as if he passed his life perpetually walking backward through a desert, sweeping away his footprints, leaving him with only scattered recollections of rough lips pressed against his, and the comfort of a man's muscular weight.

"I love you," he said.

Marcus did not roll over or look behind him, did not say "I love you" in return, and indeed, said nothing at all. The ticking of Parrish's antique grandfather clock grew louder and louder with each second, and by the time the patter of rain on the roof was distinct, Liem was fumbling awkwardly with his underwear.

"Can you just wait a minute?" Marcus said, turning around and hooking one leg over Liem's body. "Don't you think you're overreacting?"

"No," Liem said, trying to unpry, without success, Marcus's leg, honed by countless hours on the treadmill and the squat machine. "I need to go to the bathroom, please."

"You just got caught by surprise. Sooner or later you'll figure out love's just a reflex action some of us have." Marcus stroked Liem's hand. "A week from now you're not even going to know why you told me that."

"Okay," he said, not sure whether he wanted to believe Marcus or not. "Sure."

"You know what else is in your future?"

"Do not—don't tell me."

"A year from now you'll be the one hearing other men say they love you," Marcus said. "They'll say you're too pretty to be alone."

Marcus pulled him closer, and, as the rain continued to fall, they held each other. Outside a car began honking repeatedly, a sound Liem knew by now to mean that someone, double-parked, was blocking the narrow street in front of the house. Then all was quiet but for the clock, and he thought Marcus might have dozed off until he stirred and said, "Aren't you going to read the letter?"

He'd forgotten about the airmail, but now that Marcus had mentioned it, he felt it glowing in the darkened living room, bearing on its blue face the oil of his father's touch, and perhaps his mother's too, the airmail the only thing he owned that truly mattered.

"I never read it to you."

"I *will never* read it to you. That's the future tense."

"*I'll* never read you the letter."

"Now you're being petty. Don't read it to me, then."

"But I *will* tell you what *I'll* write."

"Only if you want to," Marcus said, yawning.

Until this moment, Liem hadn't thought about what he would write to his father and mother once their letter had arrived. So he improvised, beginning with how the tone would be as important as the content. His letter, he said, would be a report from an exotic city, one with a Spanish name, famous for cable cars, Alcatraz Island, and the Golden Gate Bridge. He would include postcards of the tourist sights, and he'd mention how funny it was to live in a city where people who weren't even Asian knew about the autumn festival. When enormous crowds in Chinatown celebrated the lunar new year, he'd be there, throwing down firecrackers at the feet of a dancing lion, hoping his family was doing the same. The crunch of burned firecrackers under his feet would remind him of his boyhood at home, and the letter he'd write would remind him of times when the family gathered around his father as he read, aloud, the occasional note from a distant relative. At the end, Liem would tell them not to worry about him, because, he'd write, I'm working hard to save money, I'm even making friends. And we live in a mauve house.

He heard the steady rise and fall of Marcus's breathing, and, afraid Marcus was fading into sleep, he couldn't stop himself from asking the other question he'd wanted to ask since the previous day. "Tell me something," he said. Marcus's eyes fluttered and opened. "Am I good?"

A light drizzle tapped against the windows, the sound of Friday night on a rainy day. "Yes," Marcus said, closing his eyes once more. "You were very good."

This much, at least, he could write home about.

After Marcus fell asleep, Liem slid out of bed and went to the bathroom, where he stood under a spray of hot water for so long he nearly fainted from the heat and steam. He had his pants on and was combing his hair when the phone rang in the living room.

"I just wanted to see how you two were doing," Parrish said, loud and cheerful, as if he'd been out drinking.

"Just fine," Liem said, eyeing the letter on the coffee table. "Nothing special." He didn't like speaking on the phone, where body language was no help in making himself understood, and he kept the conversation short. Parrish didn't seem to mind, and said good night just as boisterously as he'd said hello.

Liem sat down on the couch and opened the letter carefully. When he unfolded the single sheet of onionskin paper, translucent in the light, he recognized once again his father's script, awkward and loopy, as hard for him to decipher as it was for his father to write.

September 20, 1975

Dear son,

We got your airmail yesterday. Everyone's so happy to know you're alive and well. We're all fine. This summer, your uncles and cousins were reeducated with the other enlisted puppet soldiers. The Party forgave their crimes. Your uncles were so grateful, they donated their houses to the revolution. Our lives are more joyful now that your uncles, your cousins, and their wives and children are living with us in our house. The cadres tell us that we will erase the past and rebuild our glorious country!

When you have time, send us the news from America. It must be more sinful even than Saigon, so remember what the cadres say. The revolutionary man must live a civil, healthy, correct life! We all think of you often. Your mother misses you, and sends you her love. So do I.

Your Father

After he read the letter a second time, he folded it, slid it back into its envelope, and let it lie inert on the coffee table. Restless, he stood up and walked over to the bay window overlooking the street and the sidewalks, empty this late in the evening. The light in the room had turned the window into a mirror, superimposing his likeness over the landscape outside. When he raised his hand, his reflection raised its hand, and when he touched his face, the reflection did the same, and when he traced the curve of his cheek and the line of his jaw, so, too, did the mirror image. Why, then, did he not recognize himself? And why did he see right through himself to the dark street outside?

Raindrops on the glass dappled the reflection of his face. He waited at the streaky window for several minutes until he saw a sign of life, two men striding quickly down the street, shoulders occasionally brushing and hands deep in the pockets of their jackets. Their heads, ducked down low against the drizzle, were bent toward each other at a slight angle as each listened to what the other was saying. At one time he would have thought the two men could only be friends. Now he saw they could easily be lovers.

As they passed under a streetlamp, one of them said something that made the other laugh, his head tilting back so that his unremarkable face was illuminated for a second. The man's eyes turned to Liem at that instant, and Liem, realizing he was quite visible from the street, wondered what kind of figure he must have cut, bare-chested and arms akimbo, his hair slicked back. Suddenly the man raised his hand, as if to say hello. When his partner looked toward the window as well, Liem waved in return, and for a moment there were only the three of them, sharing a fleeting connection. Then the men passed by, and long after they had vanished into the shadows he was still standing with his hand pressed to the window, wondering if someone, behind blinds and curtains, might be watching.

WAR YEARS

*B*efore Mrs. Hoa broke into our lives in the summer of 1983, nothing my mother did surprised me. Her routine was as predictable as the rotation of the earth, beginning with how she rapped on my door every morning, at six, six fifteen, and six thirty, until at last I was awake. When I emerged from my bedroom, she was already dressed, invariably wearing a short-sleeved blouse and skirt of matching pastels. She owned seven such outfits, and if she had on fuchsia, I knew it was Monday. Before we departed, she switched off the lights, checked the burners, tugged on the black iron grills guarding our windows, always in that order, and then, in the car, ordered me to lock my door.

As my father steered the Oldsmobile and I sat in the back reading a comic book, my mother worked on her makeup. By the time we arrived at St. Patrick ten minutes later, she was finished, the flags of blush on her cheeks blending in with her foundation. Perfume was the last touch, a pump of the spray on either side of her neck. The dizzying scent of gardenias clung to me in Ms. Korman's summer school classroom, where, for seven hours every day, I spoke only English. I liked school, even summer school. It was like being on vacation from home, and at three o'clock, I was always a little disappointed to walk the four blocks to the grocery store my parents owned, the New Saigon Market, where English was hardly ever spoken and Vietnamese was loud.

My mother and father rarely left their posts, the cash registers flanking the entrance of the New Saigon. Customers always crowded the market, one of the few places in San Jose where the Vietnamese could buy the staples and spices of home, jasmine rice and star anise, fish sauce and fire-engine-red chilies. People haggled endlessly with my mother over everything, beginning with the rock sugar, which I pretended was yellow kryptonite, and ending with the varieties of meat in the freezer, from pork chops and catfish with a glint of light in their eyes to shoestrings of chewy tripe and packets of chicken hearts, small and tender as button mushrooms.

"Can't we just sell TV dinners?" I asked once. It was easy to say *TV dinners* in Vietnamese since the word for television was *ti-vi*, but there were no Vietnamese words for other things I wanted. "And what about bologna?"

"What?" My mother's brow furrowed. "If I can't pronounce it, my customers won't buy it. Now go stamp the prices on those cans."

"They're just going to ask for a lower price." I was thirteen, beginning to be brave enough to say what I had suspected for a while, that my mother wasn't always right. "Why do they haggle over everything? Why can't they just pay the price that's there?"

"Are you going to be the kind of person who always pays the asking price?" my mother demanded. "Or the kind who fights to find out what something's really worth?"

I wasn't sure. All I knew was that in the New Saigon, my chore every afternoon was to price the cans and packages. I was on my knees, rummaging for the stamp pad on the shelf behind my mother, when Mrs. Hoa introduced herself. Like my mother, she was in her late forties and dressed in monochrome, a white jacket, white pants, and white shoes, with bug-eyed sunglasses obscuring her face. As my mother bagged her purchases, Mrs. Hoa said, "I'm collecting funds for the fight against the Communists, my dear." I knew the basics of our history as well as I knew the story of Adam and Eve: the Communists had marched from North Vietnam in 1975 to invade South Vietnam, driving us out, all the way across the Pacific to California. I had no memories of the war, but Mrs. Hoa said others had not forgotten. A guerrilla army of former South Vietnamese soldiers was training in the jungles of Thailand, preparing to launch a counterattack in unified Vietnam. The plan was to stir the unhappy people against their Communist rulers, incite a revolution, and resurrect the Republic of the South.

"Our men need our support," Mrs. Hoa said. "And we need good citizens like yourself to contribute."

My mother rubbed one ankle against the other, her nylons scratching. A seam had opened behind her knee, but my mother would keep wearing the same hose until the run nipped at her heels. "I wish I could help, Mrs. Hoa, but times are hard," my mother said. "Our customers are cutting back on everything, what with the recession and the gas prices. And our daughter's in college. Her tuition is like a down payment on a house every year."

"I struggle making ends meet, too." Mrs. Hoa unclasped and clasped the silver latch on her purse. A thin gold band encircled her ring finger, and the red enamel on her nails was as polished and glossy as a new car's paint. "But people talk. Did you hear about Mrs. Binh? People say she's a Communist sympathizer, and all because she's too cheap to give anything. There's even talk of boycotting her store."

My mother knew Mrs. Binh, owner of Les Amis Beauty Salon a few blocks farther west downtown, but changed the topic to the steamy June weather and the price of gold. Mrs. Hoa agreed about the temperature, smiling and displaying a formidable wall of teeth. She glanced at me before leaving my mother with this: "Think about it, dear. Taking back our homeland is a noble cause for which we should all be proud to fight."

"Idiot," my mother muttered after Mrs. Hoa was gone. As we drove home that evening along Tenth Street, my mother recounted the episode to my father, who had been too busy at his own register to overhear the conversation. When she mentioned the guerrillas, I imagined them to be unshaven, mosquito-bitten men with matted hair wearing ragged tiger-stripe fatigues; living on rainwater, wild boar, and aphids; practicing hand-to-hand combat skills by bayoneting jackfruit. From the backseat, I said, "How much are you giving Mrs. Hoa?"

"Nothing," she replied. "It's extortion."

"But they're fighting the Communists," I said. Also known as Chinese and North Koreans, with Cubans and Sandinistas threatening infiltration and invasion from south of our border, as President Reagan explained on *World News Tonight*. "Shouldn't we help them?"

"The war's over." My mother sounded tired. "There's no fighting it again."

I was outraged, for Mrs. Hoa's appearance proved the war was not over, in that she had somehow followed us from the old Saigon to the new one. What was more, I had read *Newsweek* in the dentist's office and knew we were in the midst of an epic battle against the evil empire of the Soviet Union. But if I was unhappy with my mother's response, I was even more upset with my father's.

"The war may be over," he said, wiggling his little finger in his ear, "but paying a little hush money would make our lives a lot easier."

My mother said nothing, merely drumming her fingers on the armrest. I knew she would have her way with my father, a bald man with the deliberate moves and patient eyes of a turtle. Late that night, hurrying from the kitchen to my room with a glass of water, I heard my mother working to persuade him behind their closed door. There was no time to eavesdrop. We had recently read "The Fall of the House of Usher" in Ms. Korman's class, and the fear of seeing someone undead in the dark hallway made me rush past their door, just as my mother said, "I've dealt with worse than her."

Dread was stronger than curiosity. I shut my door and jumped into bed shivering, pushing aside my summer textbooks, which were wrapped in brown covers I had cut from a shopping bag and upon which I had scrawled "Math" and "American History." Perhaps my mother was talking about the famine at the end of the Second World War, when she was nine. Last year, an evening television report on the Ethiopian famine had prompted my mother to mention this other famine while I plucked the gray hairs from her head. "Do you know a dozen children in my village starved to death?" she said, even though I obviously did not know. "Older people, too, sometimes right on the street. One day I found a girl I used to play with dead on her doorstep." My mother lapsed into silence as she stared at a point on the wall above the television, and I did not say anything. It was the kind of story she told all the time, and in any case, I was too distracted to ask questions. She was paying me for every strand I found and I was intent on my search, each gray hair bringing me one nickel closer to the next issue of *Captain America*.

In the days and nights that passed, my mother never brought up Mrs. Hoa, but the woman had unsettled her. My mother began talking during our evening bookkeeping, a time when she was usually completely focused on calculating the daily receipts. We worked at the dining table, counting cash, rolling coins into paper packages the size of firecrackers, and stamping the New Saigon's address onto the back of the personal checks, the Monopoly-money food stamps, and the yellow coupons from Aid to Families with Dependent Children. When I added the sums with a humming mechanical calculator bigger than our rotary telephone, I never needed to look at the keypad. I knew every number's place by heart. It would be the only time I was ever good at math.

As we did the day's reckoning, my mother reported on the rumors of former South Vietnamese soldiers organizing not only a guerrilla army in Thailand but also a secret front here in the United States, its purpose to overthrow the Communists. Grimmer than rumors was how unknown assailants had firebombed a Vietnamese newspaper editor's office in Garden Grove (he died), while another editor had been shot to death, along with his wife, in the doorway of their house in Virginia (the murderers were never caught). "They just said in public what a lot of people already say in private," my mother said, wetting her fingers on a sponge. "Making peace with the Communists might not be such a bad thing."

I wrote down figures in a ledger, never looking up. My father and I worked in T-shirts and shorts, but my mother wore only a nightgown of sheer green fabric without a bra. She wasn't aware of how her breasts swayed like anemones under shallow water, embarrassing me whenever I saw those dark and doleful areolas with their nipples as thick as my index finger. My mother's breasts were nothing like those of the girls in my class, or so I imagined in fantasies that had been confirmed the week before when I had seen Emmy Tsuchida's nipple through the gap between two buttons of her shirt, pink and pert, exactly like the eraser on the pencil in my hand. Without raising my gaze from the ledger, I said, "But you always tell me the Communists are bad people."

"O-ho!" my father said with a chortle. "So you do pay attention. Sometimes I can't tell what's going on behind those thick glasses of yours."

"The Communists are evil." My mother riffled through a stack of twenty-dollar bills. She had never finished grade school, her father forcing her to stay at home to care for her siblings, and yet she could count money by hand and add figures in her head more quickly than I could on the calculator. "There's no doubt about it. They don't believe in God and they don't believe in money."

"But they believe in taking other people's money," my father said. He spoke often of his auto parts store, which according to his brothers no longer had any parts to sell under Communist ownership. We had lived above the store, and sometimes I wondered if a Communist child was sleeping in my bed, and if so, what kinds of books a Red read, and what kind of movies he saw. *Captain America* was out of the question, but he must have seen Luke Skywalker crossing light sabers with Darth Vader. I had seen *Star Wars* a dozen times on videotape, and if anyone was so deprived as to have not watched it even once, then the country in which he lived surely needed a revolution. But my mother would not have agreed. She wrapped a paper band around the twenties and said, "I hate the Communists as much as Mrs. Hoa, but she's fighting a war that can't be won. I'm not throwing away my money on a lost cause."

My father ended the conversation by standing and sweeping the cash, coins, checks, and food stamps into the vinyl satchel he carried every morning to the Bank of America. My parents kept some of their profits in the bank, donated a portion to the church, and wired another percentage to the relatives in Vietnam, who periodically mailed us thin letters thick with trouble, summed up for me by my mother to the tune of no food and no money, no school and no hope. Their relatives' experiences and their own had taught my parents to believe that no country was immune to disaster, and so they secreted another percentage of the profits at home, just in case some horrendous calamity wiped out the American banking system. My mother wrapped blocks of hundred-dollar bills in plastic and taped them underneath the lid of the toilet tank, buried dog-tag-sized ounces of gold in the rice, and stashed her jade bracelets, twenty-four-karat gold necklaces, and diamond rings in a portable fireproof safe, hidden in the crawl space underneath the house. To distract thieves, she devised decoys, placing a large glass vase heavy with coins high on a bookshelf by the front door, and a pair of gold bracelets on top of her dresser.

Her fear of robbery was proved justified last October, when, on an otherwise forgettable Tuesday evening, someone knocked on the door. My father was in the kitchen, having just turned on the stove, and I reached the door a few steps ahead of my mother, already in her nightgown. When I peered through the peephole, I saw a white man who said, "I got mail for you, sir." If he had spoken in Vietnamese or Spanish, I never would have unlocked the door, but because he spoke English, I did. He used his left hand to push his way into the house, a young man in his twenties with feathered hair the color of old straw, long enough to brush the collar of his frayed jeans jacket. Not much taller than my mother, he was slightly built; when he spoke, his voice squeaked like rubber soles on a gym floor.

"Get back," he said. His forehead was slick with sweat, and in his right hand was a gun. Even with the passage of decades, I can still see that gun clearly, a black-barreled .22 revolver that he waved before him with a trembling hand as he stepped past the threshold, kicking at the jumble of shoes we kept there and forgetting to close the door. My mother concluded later that he was an amateur, perhaps an addict desperate for money. He pointed the gun past me, at her, and said, "You understand English? Get on the floor!"

I backed away, while my mother threw her hands in the air, saying, "*Khong, khong, khong!*" My father had appeared, halfway between the kitchen and the front door, and the man fixed his aim on him, saying, "Get down, mister." My father got onto his knees, raising his hands high. "No shoot," my father said in English, his voice faint. "No shoot, please."

I had never seen my father on his knees outside church, and I had never seen my mother tremble and shake with fear.

Pity overwhelmed me; I knew this was neither the first nor the last time someone would humiliate them like this. As if aware of my thoughts, the man pointed the gun at me wordlessly, and I got down on my knees, too. Only my mother did not sink to her knees, her back against the wall and her face, freshly peeled of makeup, very white. Her breasts undulated behind her nightgown, like the heads of twin eels, as she kept saying *no*. The man was still aiming his gun at me as he said, "What's her problem, kid?"

When my mother screamed, the sound froze everyone except her. She pushed past the man, nudging the gun aside with her hand and bumping him with her shoulder as she ran outside. He stumbled against the bookshelf by the door, knocking over the glass vase full of coins. Falling to the ground, it shattered, spraying pennies, nickels, and dimes all over, the coins mixed with shards of glass. "Jesus Christ!" the man said. When he turned toward the door, my father leaped up and hurled himself against the man's back, shoving him across the threshold and then slamming the door shut. Outside, the gun went off with a short, sharp little *pop*, the bullet ricocheting off the sidewalk and lodging itself in the wall next to the mailbox, where a policeman would dig it out a few hours later.

On Sunday morning before we left for church, my mother used a dab of Brylcreem and a black Ace comb to slick my hair and part it down the middle. I was horrified at the way

I looked, like Alfalfa from *Little Rascals*, but I didn't protest, just as I hadn't said anything to her after the police brought my mother back home from a neighbor's house. "I saved our lives, you coward!" she yelled at my father, who smiled weakly at the police sergeant taking down our report while we sat at the dining table. To me, as she yanked my ear, she said, "What did I say about opening the door to strangers? How come you never listen to me?" When the police sergeant asked me to translate, I rubbed my ear and said, "She's just scared, officer."

The police never caught the man, and, after a while, there was no more reason to mention him. Even so, I thought about him every now and again, especially on Sunday mornings during mass when I rose from kneeling. It was then that I remembered how I had gotten off my knees to see my mother dashing by the living room window, barefoot on the sidewalk before all the people in their cars, hands raised high in the air and wearing only her nightgown in the twilight, shouting something I could not hear. She had saved us, and wasn't salvation always the message from our priest, Father Dinh? According to my mother, he was already middle-aged when he led his flock, including my parents, from the north of Vietnam to the south in 1954, after the Communists had kicked out the French and seized the northern half of the country. Fantastically, Father Dinh still had more hair than my father, a tuft of white thread that shone under the light illuminating the stained glass windows. His voice trembled when he said, "In the name of the Father, the Son, and the Holy Spirit," and I could not help dozing in the hard-backed pew while he sermonized, remembering Emmy Tsuchida's nipple and looking forward only to the end of mass.

It was in the crowd jostling for the exit that Mrs. Hoa touched my mother's elbow one Sunday, a few weeks after the break-in. "Didn't you enjoy the father's sermon?" Mrs. Hoa said. Her eyes were curiously flat, as if painted onto her face. My mother's back stiffened, and she barely turned her head to say, "I liked it very much."

"I haven't heard from you yet about your donation, dear. Next week, perhaps? I'll come by." Mrs. Hoa was dressed formally, in an *ao dai* of midnight velvet embroidered with a golden lotus over the breast. It must have been unbearably hot in summer weather, but no perspiration showed on her temples. "Meanwhile, here's something to read."

She produced a sheet of paper from her purse, the same fake alligator skin one with the silver clasp I'd seen last week, and offered it to me. The mimeograph was in Vietnamese, which I could not read, but the blurry photograph said it all, gaunt men standing at attention in rank and file under fronds of palm trees, wearing exactly the tiger-stripe fatigues I'd imagined.

"What a handsome boy." Mrs. Hoa's tone was unconvincing. She wore the same white high heels I'd seen before. "And you said your daughter's in college?"

"On the East Coast."

"Harvard? Yale?" Those were the only two East Coast schools the Vietnamese knew. My mother, who could not pronounce Bryn Mawr, said, "Another one."

"What's she studying? Law? Medicine?"

My mother looked down in shame when she said, "Philosophy." She had scolded my sister Loan during her Christmas vacation, telling her she was wasting her education. My father had agreed, saying, "Everyone needs a doctor or a lawyer, but who needs a philosopher? We can get advice for free from the priest."

Mrs. Hoa smiled once more and said, "Excellent!" After she was gone, I handed the mimeograph to my mother, who shoved it into her purse. In the parking lot, crammed with cars and people, my mother pinched my father and said, "I'm following Mrs. Hoa. You and Long run the market by yourselves for a few hours."

My father grimaced and rubbed his hand over his head. "And what, exactly, are you planning to do?"

"She knows where we work. I'll bet she knows where we live. It's only fair I know the same things, isn't it?"

"Okay." My father sighed. "Let's go, son."

"I want to go with Ma."

"You, too?" my father muttered.

I was curious about Mrs. Hoa, and helping my mother was an excuse not to spend my morning at the New Saigon. My mother and I followed her in our Oldsmobile, heading south. Mrs. Hoa drove a small Datsun sedan the color of an egg yolk, peppered with flakes of rust. Superimposed upon the Datsun was the Virgin Mary, her image reflected in the windshield from her picture on the dash, as dim as our handful of fading color photos from Vietnam. My favorite featured a smiling young couple sitting on a grassy slope in front of a pink country church, Ba in his sunglasses as he embraced Ma, who wore a peach *ao dai* over silk cream pants, her abundant hair whipped into a bouffant.

"*Nam xu*," my mother said, turning left onto Story Road. Thinking she wanted a translation into English, I said, "A nickel?"

"Five cents is my profit on a can of soup." As my mother drove, she kept her foot on the brake, not the accelerator. My head bounced back and forth on the headrest like a ball tethered to a paddle. "Ten cents for a pound of pork, twenty-five cents for ten pounds of rice. That woman wants five hundred dollars from me, but you see how we fight for each penny?"

"Uh-huh," I said, beads of sweat trickling from my armpit. Looking back so many decades later, I wonder if she was exaggerating or if I am now, my memory attempting to approximate what our lives felt like. But I am certain that when I rolled down the window and flung out my hand to surf the breeze, my mother said, "A bus might come along and rip your arm off." I pulled my arm back in and sighed. I yearned for the woman she once was in that old photograph, when my sister and I were not yet born and the war was nowhere to be seen, when my mother and father owned the future. Sometimes I tried to imagine what she looked like when she was even younger, at nine, and I could not. Without a photo, my mother as a little girl no longer existed anywhere, perhaps not even in her own mind. More than all those people starved by famine, it was the thought of my mother not remembering what she looked like as a little girl that saddened me.

Mrs. Hoa turned off Story Road onto a side street, a neighborhood of one-story homes with windows too small for the walls. Well-worn Ford pickups and Chrysler lowriders with chrome rims were parked on the lawns. The front yard of Mrs. Hoa's house was paved over, and her yellow Datsun joined a white Toyota Corolla with a crushed bumper and a green Honda Civic missing a hubcap. After Mrs. Hoa walked inside, my mother cruised forward to inspect the house, painted with a newish coat of cheap, bright turquoise, the garage transformed into a storefront with sliding glass doors and a red neon sign that said NHA MAY. The blinds on the tailor shop's windows and the curtains of the living room were drawn, showing their white backs. The man who had invaded our house must have followed us home in the same way, but my mother did not seem to recognize this. Instead, her voice was full of satisfaction when she spoke. "Now," she said, easing her foot off the brake, "we know where she lives."

When Mrs. Hoa came to the New Saigon on Wednesday afternoon of the following week, I was in the wooden loft my father had hammered together above the kitchenware at the rear of the store. We stored enough long-grain rice in the loft to feed a village, stacked nearly to the ceiling in burlap sacks of ten, twenty-five, and fifty pounds. The clean carpet scent of jasmine rice permeated the air as I sat astride a dike of rice sacks, reading about Reconstruction. I had reached the part about the scalawags and carpetbaggers who had come from the North to help rebuild, or perhaps swindle, the South, when I saw Mrs. Hoa at the doorway, wearing the white outfit from her first visit.

By the way my mother gripped the sides of the cash register as if it were a canoe rocking in the waves while Mrs. Hoa talked to her, I knew there would be trouble. I climbed down the ladder, made my way past aisles stocked with condensed milk and cellophane noodles, shrimp chips and dried cuttlefish, lychees and green mangoes, ducking my head to avoid the yellow strips of sticky flypaper dangling from the ceiling, and reached the front of the store as my mother was saying, "I'm not giving you any money." A crack showed in her foundation, a line creasing her cheek from nose to jawbone. "I work hard for my money. What do you do? You're nothing but a thief and an extortionist, making people think they can still fight this war."

I stood behind a row of customers, one of them reading the same mimeograph Mrs. Hoa gave me in church. Mrs. Hoa's face had turned as white as her outfit, and red lipstick smeared her ochre teeth, bared in fury. She glared at the customers and said, "You heard her, didn't you? She doesn't support the cause. If she's not a Communist, she's just as bad as a Communist. If you shop here, you're helping Communists."

Mrs. Hoa slammed a stack of mimeographs onto the counter by the register, and with that, she left. My mother stared at my father at the register across from her, and neither said a word as the Datsun sputtered into life outside. The customers in front of me shifted uneasily. Within an hour, they would be on their telephones, all telling their friends, who in turn would tell their friends, who then would tell more people, until everyone in the community knew. My mother turned to the customers with her face as carefully composed as the letters she sent to her relatives, showing no signs of worry, and said, "Who's next?"

Throughout the rest of the day, my mother made no mention of Mrs. Hoa, and I thought that she would simply ignore her, hoping she would not return. But the moment we got into the car, my mother began talking about her counterattack, and I realized that she had been simmering for hours, keeping quiet for the sake of the customers. My mother would go to Mrs. Hoa and demand an apology, for her accusation could cost my mother her reputation and her business, given the depth of anti-Communist fervor in our Vietnamese community. My mother would call Mrs. Hoa a disgrace and slap her if she refused. My mother would point out the hopelessness and self-delusion of Mrs. Hoa's cause, reducing her to tears with logic. As my mother rehearsed her plans, my father said nothing, and neither did I. We knew better than to oppose her, and when we reached our house, he went wordlessly inside to start dinner, as instructed. My mother drove on to Mrs. Hoa's house, taking me with her because, she said, "That woman won't do anything crazy with you there."

It was eight thirty when my mother parked the car in Mrs. Hoa's driveway, behind the Datsun. Mrs. Hoa answered the door wearing an orange tank top and a pair of shorts in a purple floral print. Her hair was pinned back in a bun and her face, bereft of mascara, lipstick, or foundation was creviced, pitted, and cracked—it belonged to a woman years older. Her small breasts were no bigger than those of Emmy Tsuchida, and a map of varicose veins on her skinny thighs and shins led south to gnarled toes, the yellowing nails spotted with red dabs of chipped polish.

"What are you doing here?" Mrs. Hoa said.

"I want to speak to you," my mother said. "Aren't you going to invite us in?"

Mrs. Hoa hesitated and then stepped back begrudgingly. We took off our shoes and picked our way past the loafers, sneakers, pumps, and flip-flops jammed around the door. Racks on wheels, crammed with hangers for girls' clothes, hid the window, while a pair of bunk beds ran along two walls of the living room. In the center was a long folding table, stacked with notebooks and textbooks.

"We're having dinner," Mrs. Hoa said. Other voices rang from the dining room. An aerosol of grease clung to the air, along with the warm, wet sock odor of cooked rice. "Have you eaten yet?"

"Yes." If my mother was surprised at Mrs. Hoa's politeness, she didn't show it. "I'd like to talk in private."

Mrs. Hoa shrugged and led us past the dining room. At the packed table sat eight or nine people with heads turned our way, little girls with bowl cuts, a quartet of grandparents, and a man and woman around my mother's age, the shadows under their eyes so pronounced they looked as if someone had punched them again and again. Just as crowded was Mrs. Hoa's bedroom, the first one down the hall. An industrial steel-frame table, a sewing machine fastened to it, dominated the middle of the room, while the velvet *ao dai* and the white jacket and pants hung from the bunk bed, blocking the window. Mrs. Hoa sat on the only chair, behind the sewing machine, and said, "What do you want?"

My mother glanced at the closet, doors removed to reveal hand-built pine shelves stacked with bolts of silk and cotton. One of the two clothing racks behind Mrs. Hoa was hung with everyday clothing—women's slacks and blouses, men's suits and dress shirts—while the other was hung with uniforms, olive-green fatigues and camouflage outfits patterned with blotches of brown, black, and green in varying shades, the same kind issued to the marines who had liberated Grenada not long ago. My mother said, "You tailor uniforms for the soldiers?"

"American sizes are too large for Vietnamese men and the proportions aren't right. Plus the men want their names sewn on, and their ranks and units." Mrs. Hoa reached under the sewing table and lifted a cardboard box, and when we leaned over the table to peek inside, we saw plastic sandwich bags filled with chevrons and the colorful badges of Vietnamese units. "Some of these uniforms are for the guerrilla army in Thailand, but others are for our men here."

I wondered if she meant the rumored secret front, or the men my father's age and younger that I saw at Tet festivals, veterans of the vanquished South Vietnamese army who welcomed the New Year by wearing military uniforms and checking tickets at the fairgrounds where the festivals happened.

"Your husband's a soldier?" my mother said.

"He's a commando. The CIA parachuted him into the north in 1963. I haven't heard from him since." Mrs. Hoa spoke without any change in inflection, clutching the box to her chest. "The Americans sent my younger son's division to Laos in 1972. He never returned. As for my eldest son, he was in the army, too. The Communists killed him. I buried him in Bien Hoa in 1969. My daughter wrote to tell me the Communists scratched the eyes out of the picture on his grave."

My mother was silent, fingering a tiger-stripe camouflage jacket hanging from the rack. At last, she said, "I'm sorry to hear about your husband and your sons."

"Sorry for what?" Mrs. Hoa's voice was shrill. "Whoever said my husband was dead? No one saw him die. No one saw my youngest son die, either. They're alive, and no one like you is going to tell me otherwise."

I studied the patterns in the beige carpet, shapes of a frog and a tree, trapped there along with odors of garlic and sesame, sweat and moisturizer. My mother broke the silence by opening her purse and digging inside. From the crumpling of paper, I knew she was opening the envelope with the day's cash. She extracted two hundred-dollar bills and laid them on the sewing table in front of Mrs. Hoa, smoothing the face of Benjamin Franklin on each bill, the same way she ran her palm over my hair before entering church.

"That's it," my mother said. "That's all I have."

I calculated the cans of soup, the pounds of rice, and the hours of standing on her feet that made those two hundred dollars possible, and I was astonished that my mother had surrendered the money. When Mrs. Hoa looked at the cash, I thought she might demand the five hundred dollars she'd asked for, but she swept up the bills, folded them, and dropped them into the box on her lap. As she and my mother stared at each other after that, I thought about how years ago my mother had bribed a general's wife with an ounce of gold, buying my father's freedom from the draft. My mother had mentioned the incident one night to my father as they inspected another ounce they had just purchased, and he, glancing at me, had said, "Let's not talk about that." They would file this incident with Mrs. Hoa under the same category of things better left unspoken.

"We'll see ourselves out," my mother said.

"You see how the Communists weren't satisfied with killing my son once?" Mrs. Hoa aimed her gaze at me. "They killed him twice when they desecrated his grave. They don't respect anybody, not even the dead."

Her voice was urgent, and when she suddenly leaned forward, I was afraid she was going to reach across the sewing machine and grasp my hand. I willed myself not to back away from her fingers, two of them bandaged as if she had pricked herself with needles. I felt that I had to say something, and so I said, "I'm sorry." I meant that I was sorry for all that had happened, not only to her but also to my mother, the accumulation of everything I could do nothing about. My apology made utterly no difference, but Mrs. Hoa nodded gravely, as if understanding my intentions. In a subdued tone, she said, "I know you are."

Those were her last words to me. She did not say goodbye when we left, and indeed, did not even look at us, for as my mother closed the bedroom door, Mrs. Hoa was gazing down into the box, her bent head revealing a furrow of white roots running through her scalp, where the hair's natural color revealed itself along a receding tide of black dye. It was a trivial secret, but one I would remember as vividly as my feeling that while some people are haunted by the dead, others are haunted by the living.

When my mother exited the freeway, she surprised me for the second time. She pulled into the parking lot of the 7-Eleven off the exit, two blocks from home, and said, "You've been such a good boy. Let's get you a treat." I didn't know what to say. My parents did not grant me so much as an allowance. When I had asked for one in the fourth grade, my father had frowned and said, "Let me think it over." The next night he handed me an itemized list of expenses that included my birth, feeding, education, and clothing, the sum total being $24,376. "This doesn't include emotional aggravation, compound interest, or future expenses," my father said. "Now when can you start paying *me* an allowance?"

My mother stopped under the bright lights at the door of the 7-Eleven, pulled a crisp five-dollar bill out of her purse, and handed it to me. "Go buy," she said in English, motioning me inside. Whenever she spoke in English, her voice took on a higher pitch, as if instead of coming from inside her, the language was outside, squeezing her by the throat. "Anything you want."

I left her on the sidewalk and went in, the five-dollar bill as slick as wax paper in my hand, remembering how my mother's lips moved whenever she used the fingers of one hand to count on the fingers of her other hand. The 7-Eleven was empty except for the two Sikh men at the registers, who gave me bored looks and returned to their conversation. Disinfectant tinted the air. I ignored the bank of arcade games and the racks of comic books, even though the covers of *Superman* and *Iron Man* caught my eye and the electronic whirring of Pac-Man called to me. Past the cleaning products and canned soups was an aisle stocked with chips, cookies, and candy. I glanced down the aisle, saw the glint of gold foil on a chocolate bar, and froze. While the clerks chatted in a language I could not understand, I hesitated, yearning to take everything home but unable to choose.

72

THE TRANSPLANT

Many unexpected things had happened to Arthur Arellano, and the transformation of his modest garage into a warehouse, stacked with boxes upon cardboard boxes of counterfeit goods, was far from the most surprising. Written on the boxes were names like Chanel, Versace, and Givenchy, designers of luxuries far beyond the reach of Arthur and his wife, Norma. Their presence made Arthur uneasy, and so it was that in the week after Louis Vu delivered this unforeseen wealth to the Arellanos, Arthur found himself slipping out of his rented house at odd hours, stealing down the pebbly driveway past his Chevy Nova, and opening the garage door to ponder the goods with which he was now living so intimately.

Even under the cover of night, Arthur resisted the urge to pocket a Prada wallet or a pair of Yves Saint Laurent cuff links, even though Louis ended nearly every phone call by saying, "Help yourself." But Arthur could not help himself, for he was troubled by a lingering sense of guilt and a fear of the law, trepidations that Louis addressed during their weekly lunch at Brodard's, where, under Louis's tutelage, Arthur had cultivated a keen taste for Vietnamese fare. According to Louis, Brodard's was the finest example of such cuisine in the Little Saigon of Orange County. As Arthur ate the first course on their most recent visit, a succulent salad of rare beef sliced paper-thin and marinated in lemon and ginger grass, a cousin to the ceviche he loved, he wondered how the same dish would taste in Vietnam. Usually Louis would hold forth on how the dishes at Brodard's were even tastier than those in the homeland itself, but as the waiter cleared away the plate, Louis chose another subject: why his business did more good than harm.

"It's like beautiful people and ugly people," Louis said. "Beautiful people can't let on that they need ugly people. But without the ugly, the beautiful wouldn't look half so good. Am I right? Tell me I'm right."

Arthur eyed the next course the waiter was slipping onto their table, six roasted squab fetchingly arrayed on a bed of romaine lettuce. "I suppose you're right," said Arthur, whose grasp of capitalism was tenuous at best. "Those look delicious."

"The moral of the story is this," Louis said, choosing a bird for himself. "The more fakes there are, the more that people who can't buy the real things want them. And the more people buy the fakes, the more the real things are worth. Everybody wins."

"That's the way you see things," said Arthur, lifting a squab by its slender little leg. "But don't you think you're just telling yourself what you want to hear?"

"Of course I'm telling myself what I want to hear!" Louis shook his head in mock exasperation, his eyes wide behind his sculptural Dolce & Gabbana eyeglasses. "We all tell ourselves what we want to hear. The point, Arthur, is this: Do *you* want to hear what I'm telling myself?"

Arthur had indeed wanted to hear the many rhetorical questions posed by Louis over the past few months. For example, Louis had said, consider his eyeglasses, manufactured in the same factory that produced the real D & G frames, but after hours, with ghost workers whose shadow labor resulted in a product that cost two hundred dollars less. For those with limited income, didn't the right to own some Italian style trump any possible losses to Dolce & Gabbana? Or, Louis went on, think about Montblanc. Arthur had never thought about Montblanc and did not know it was a pen company until Louis told him. Did it suffer more than its workers in Wengang, China, Louis asked, if those workers could not make their replicas of the very expensive originals? Although Arthur had no idea what Wengang looked like, he could conjure up a blurry image of the faraway Chinese, dark haired, tight eyed, and nimble, somewhat like Louis himself.

"I'm hearing what you're telling me," Arthur said, watching Louis eat his squab with the bird perched between thumbs and index fingers, his pinkies pointed upward and outward. "Otherwise your things wouldn't be in our garage."

"Hopefully you've been listening and not just hearing," said Louis. "Money's to be made, Arthur. Good money."

But for all of Louis's talk of profits, Arthur and Norma had refused the ten percent commission Louis had offered. Lending Louis their garage was an act of sympathy stirred by the sight of his apartment, a one-bedroom cave doubling as a warehouse. The loan was also a way of paying back Louis's father, who had saved Arthur's life last year, however inadvertently. As Louis nibbled on the squab, Arthur was moved once more by the memory of Men Vu, a man he had never met.

"Keep those boxes in our garage," Arthur said. "Like I told you, it's our gift."

Before Louis could respond, Arthur's cell phone buzzed. The text message was from Norma: *pick up dry cleaning*. After Louis leaned over to read the message, he poked Arthur in the shoulder and said, "You should pick up some flowers for Norma as well." Arthur meant to ask what kind of flowers he should get for his wife along with her clothing, but the arrival of the bananas flambé, Arthur's favorite dessert, distracted him from doing so. Even though he had the nagging sense throughout the afternoon of there being something he needed to do, what that was he could not remember. All he could see in his mind's eye was the waiter lighting the thimble-size pitcher of rum and pouring the flaming liquor over the bananas, a spectacle that never ceased to seduce him.

* * *

The most unexpected thing to happen to Arthur Arellano, and the fateful event that brought him together with Louis Vu, was the failure of his liver, an organ to which Arthur had given much less thought than his nose, or his big toe, or even his right hand, all of which he could have lived without, however uncomfortably. Thus, when his liver began dying a premature death some eighteen months ago, Arthur was unprepared in every way except for having health insurance, courtesy of his younger brother and employer, Martín. The insurance covered his visit to Dr. P. K. Viswanathan, who explained that Arthur's liver was the unwitting victim of a disease Arthur understood only in its parts: auto, immune, hepatitis. Swiveling in his seat as he talked, the doctor said, "Autoimmune hepatitis means that your body no longer recognizes your liver as a part of itself. When this happens, your body rejects your liver."

"My body can do that?"

"Your body is a complex organism, Mr. Arellano." The doctor stopped swiveling and leaned forward, his elbows on the leather writing pad of his desk. "It can do pretty much whatever it wants."

Arthur left Dr. Viswanathan's office convinced of his imminent death. People needed far more organs than were available, and never had Arthur won anything worthwhile in his life. He was a chronic loser of bets big and small, from the thoroughbreds at Santa Anita to Pai Gow at the Commerce Casino's pay-to-play tables, his undistinguished career as a gambler culminating in the loss of the pink bungalow in Huntington Beach, miles from the shore, in which he and Norma had invested seventeen years of mortgage payments. After the bank repossessed the bungalow in the twenty-ninth year of their marriage, Norma left Arthur to live with one of their daughters and Arthur moved into Martín's house in Irvine. It was at the university hospital there, not long afterward, that he learned of his diagnosis, which explained how the problems he was having—the pain in his joints, the fatigue, the itches and skin rashes, the nausea and vomiting, the loss of appetite, all the things that Arthur blamed on the stress of his gambling debts over the past several years—were merely symptoms of a rot far deeper. But of all these signs, the one that drew Norma's attention when she came to him at Martín's house after the diagnosis was the jaundice, the creeping yellowness of his skin that compelled her to exclaim, "Why haven't you been taking care of yourself, Art?"

During the next hour in Martín's sun-saturated living room, Arthur humiliated himself twice, first by seizing Norma's hand and, without warning, bursting into tears, and second by confessing to having cashed out his life insurance policy. Norma did not ask how he had spent the money, and Arthur did not have the heart to tell her about Pechanga, the Indian casino in Temecula where he had lost seven days of his life, as well as all his money. For a long time Norma was silent, but when she sat down at last, he knew she had resigned herself to seeing him through his illness. When she put one hand on his knee and the other to his cheek, he also understood that the autoimmune hepatitis was God's sly way of keeping them together. This was the one benefit he could find in what was otherwise a disaster, the fear of which kept him awake at nights, staring into the darkness and wondering what lay beyond it, if anything. It was the first time he had ever been afraid for his life.

His one chance was the transplant. He fantasized about it the way he used to dream about winning the lottery, imagining how he would be a new man; someone kinder, more reliable, harder-working; somebody to make Norma proud. Thinking about the organ that would save his life, he invariably also thought about who the donor might be. In the months of waiting for news of a liver, he and Norma debated whether they should ask for the donor's identity if Arthur was so fortunate as to receive an organ. Sometimes, Dr. Viswanathan explained, donors or their families brushed away their right to anonymity. Eventually, however, Arthur and Norma decided in favor of letting modern medicine maintain its air of mystery and the miraculous. Thus it was not by choice but by accident that they discovered the liver's origin, a year after the operation, when Arthur was back working as an accountant for Martín at Arellano & Sons, the landscaping service founded by Arthur's father, Arturo, known by one and all as Big Art. The revelation arrived in a manila envelope from the hospital, left in the mailbox of the Spanish-style cottage that Arthur and Norma were renting from Martín at a substantial discount. Inside the envelope was a quality of life survey with the donor's name printed next to Arthur's own, courtesy of a bug in a hospital computer, as they and several dozen others eventually discovered when the scandal reached the headlines. On seeing the name, he felt a tremor run through his liver. He blamed it at first for what he thought was a delusion, but when he passed the survey to Norma, she saw the name as well.

"Could it be Korean? Like the Parks?" she asked, referring to their dry cleaners, Mr. and Mrs. Park, migrants from Incheon via Buenos Aires who spoke better Spanish than the Arellanos did. "If it's not Korean, maybe it's Japanese."

For his part, Arthur had no idea. He had trouble distinguishing one nationality of Asian names from another. He was also afflicted with a related, and very common, astigmatism wherein all Asians appeared the same. On first meeting the Parks, he had not thought that they were Korean, or even Japanese. Instead, he had fallen back on his default choice when confronted with a perplexing problem of identification regarding an Asian. "There are a lot of Chinese around here," Arthur said. "I'd bet this guy is Chinese."

In fact, Men Vu was from Vietnam, a widower and grandfather who had been killed in a hit-and-run, a story Norma discovered by sleuthing online. Faced at last with a real person and a real name, Arthur reluctantly concluded that he could not go on acting as if he did not know the origin of his transplant. As long as the donor was anonymous, Arthur was not obligated to him in any way. But now that he had a name, Arthur believed it was only right and proper to find someone, anyone, related to Men Vu to whom he could give thanks for having saved his life. Finding that person was more complicated than Arthur expected, since there was no Men Vu in the phone book, leaving him to call every Vu listed in

Orange County, of whom there were hundreds. After going through those who spoke no English, those who hung up on him, and those who uttered something rude in a foreign language, Arthur found, at last, Louis Vu, who listened without interruption and then said, with only the slightest accent, "I'm the one you're looking for, Mr. Arellano."

Louis pronounced his first name "Louie," or, as he put it, "the French way," and for their meeting provided an address ten minutes distant, in Fountain Valley, a pleasant suburb of tract homes, condominiums, and sprawling apartment complexes Arthur had always admired for its forthright and modest motto, which embodied all that Arthur had wanted for himself, Norma, and their brood. Those unassuming words were printed on a stone block situated on a meridian at the city's border, greeting Arthur, Norma, and all who entered Fountain Valley with this promise: "A Nice Place to Live."

Only when he was in his own living room that evening after a long afternoon of balancing the books at Arellano & Sons did Arthur remember what he had forgotten, just as Norma unlocked the front door. He turned off the television broadcast of the World Series of Poker, and as he explained that he had overlooked running down to Park Avenue Dry Cleaning, he discerned her unhappiness by the way she uttered "hmmm" without making eye contact, the noise vibrating somewhere down deep in her throat. She said "hmmm" when he asked her what she was cooking for dinner, and then said it again when he asked her what was for dinner the next day while she washed the dishes. Only when he stroked her back in bed, with the lights out, did she finally say something else.

"Let me make something very clear to you, Arthur." The pillow into which her face was turned muffled her voice. "Do not touch me, and do not come close to me."

"But—"

"Would it kill you to think about me for one moment in your life? Would it kill you to do something for me, just to see what it feels like?"

"It's the liver," he said, an excuse that had served him well over the past year. "I'm still getting used to it."

"No, you are not. You are completely recovered and good as new. That's the problem." Her back was still turned to him, and her breathing was labored, the way it was when she walked up more than two flights of stairs. "Art, you're fifty years old, and you act fifteen. Now go to sleep and leave me alone."

Arthur leaned his chin on Norma's shoulder and whispered, "Didn't you say we should talk more to each other?"

"Arthur Arellano." Norma shrugged off his chin. "Either you sleep in the living room, or I will."

Middle-aged bodies like Arthur's were not made for couches, and after a miserable night, Arthur gave in to a moment of weakness the next morning, calling his brother to ask for refuge. The phone was answered by Elvira Catalina Franco, his brother's Guatemalan housekeeper, who greeted him the way she'd been taught by Martín's wife, Carla: "Arellano residence. May I help you?" But when his brother said hello, Arthur discovered that he could no longer supplicate himself, for already he could foresee Martín's disapproving look, the eyes, cheeks, and lips puckering around the nose, pulled tighter together by the drawstring of Martín's facial muscles.

"I just called to say good morning," said Arthur, avoiding Norma's gaze as she entered the kitchen. "Good morning."

Martín sighed. "This isn't high school anymore, Artie," he said. "You're too old to make prank calls."

Even after Martín hung up, Arthur pretended to carry on a conversation, for Norma was behaving as if there was nobody in her kitchen while she toasted two slices of wheat bread, poured herself a cup of Yuban, read the headlines in the *Register*, and chuckled along with the KDAY disc jockeys. Arthur, hovering in the corner, sensed that he was merely a specter, already dead, acknowledged by Norma only as she brushed by him on her way out the door, saying over her shoulder, "Don't forget your pills."

He found his translucent orange prescription bottles and a glass of filtered water in their usual place, arrayed on the bedroom dresser. First he swallowed the diuretic, sipping from the glass and sighing. He hated taking most of the medications, even though the second pill, for lowering his blood pressure, was absolutely necessary, as was the third one, the immunosuppressive that ensured his aging body would get along with a liver of an even earlier vintage. Dr. Viswanathan had said that there would always be a risk of rejection, and the resulting sense of unease weighed on Arthur, the daily reminder of the alien within him that was delivered in quad-ruplicate form via these pills, even the fourth and final one that he somewhat enjoyed, the antidepressant. Although it was good for filing down his emotional rough edges, it was not as satisfying as the painkillers he had taken in the immediate months after the transplant, dots of magic that made his skin feel like cotton under his own fingers. The antidepressant only restored in him a feeling of normalcy, and why, Arthur wondered, should he need a pill for that?

Martín's behavior that morning in the office confirmed for Arthur how correct he had been in not asking for help. The office was in Martín's guesthouse, a clapboard cottage sepa-rated from the main house by a swimming pool cleaned with a robotic, stingray-like device that kept the water sapphire blue. Arthur had barely turned on the computer and begun contemplating his morning game of blackjack when Martín entered, sat on the edge of Arthur's desk with its stacks of unfiled receipts and invoices, and began going into minute detail about his family's vacation at Lake Arrowhead that weekend. "Jet Skis," Martín said. "Champagne brunch. Filet mignon. Pink sunsets." This, at least, was what Arthur heard, the office itself affecting his hearing, with everything from the brass paper clips to the art deco sconces reminding him of what his brother possessed that he did not, Arellano & Sons, bequeathed by Big Art only to Martín when Arthur's bad habits became obvious to their father.

"So, how was your weekend?" Martín said. "How are you and Norma doing?"

"We're fine." Arthur studied the computer screen, where he was being offered the chance to double down on a pair of tens. "We're doing great."

"Just thought I'd ask." When Martín rotated the platinum watch on his wrist, Arthur saw black threads of earth under his brother's fingernails. Arthur suspected Martín deliberately left the dirt there as proof of how he ventured out with the landscaping crews to trim a few hedges once every week, another sign of the saintliness that led Martín to trust, or perhaps to torment, Arthur with the accounting. "You know Norma talks to her pedicurist, who talks to Elaine, who talks to her mother, who talks to me. I don't even go looking for this, Artie. I just hear it because it's out there."

"I appreciate your concern." Arthur doubled down and drew a king and an ace, the kind of good luck that never happened when he was playing blackjack at the casinos. "But maybe the pedicurist said something different to Elaine, who said something a little different to Carla, who said something a little different to you, until you heard something a lot different from the way things are."

Martín sighed, coughed, and glanced at his watch. "We're brothers, Artie," he said, raising himself from the desk, which creaked in relief. At the door, Martín paused, as if to say something else, and then left, the absence of his considerable heft palpable, an imaginary cutout into which Arthur's own body could fit. According to Dr. Viswanathan, the donor would have been a man of roughly the same size and weight as Arthur himself, and from there, before having learned about Men Vu and meeting Louis, Arthur had conjectured that the donor might be in other ways like him too: middle-aged and graying, of a Mexican ancestry only vaguely remembered by word of mouth from ancient grandparents with faces like Easter Island statues, vulnerable to the seductions of seven-dollar all-you-can-eat Chinese buffets and sugar-glazed doughnuts pregnant with raspberry preserves, a profile also befitting Martín. Would Martín have given Arthur a spare part of himself? A kidney, say, or bone marrow? Would Arthur have done the same for Martín? The questions bothered Arthur all day, and later that evening in Louis's apartment, he gave the most honest answer he could to his friend.

"I think so," Arthur said. "I would, I think I really would."

The bones and scraps and wilted garnish of their dinner lay on the coffee table in Styrofoam containers, whisked to Louis's door every evening by the teenage son of a widow who cooked for two dozen bachelors. She used the four-burner stove in her own kitchen to conjure dishes that were, Louis said, minor masterpieces, aromatic catfish caramelized in a clay pot, tender chicken sautéed in lemongrass and chili, a deep-dish omelet of mushrooms and green onions, wok-fried morning glory studded with slivers of garlic, everything meant to be dipped in a pungent sauce that was the lifeblood of Vietnamese cooking, a distilled essence of fish imbued with the color of dawn and flecked by red chili pepper. Satiated, Louis sighed in appreciation and said, "It's like getting shot at. No one really knows what he'll do until bullets are flying."

"Really, I would," Arthur said. "Even though I can't stand him, he's still my brother."

"It's easy to say when you won't ever have to do it."

Indeed, Arthur never would. After he had bravely announced to Dr. Viswanathan that he too wished to donate his organs, the doctor had explained how the cyclosporine and corticosteroids Arthur ingested to keep his body from rejecting the liver had ruined his body for donation. Secretly Arthur was pleased, feeling that his decision to donate, before he was told he could not, gave him a toehold on the moral high ground, the kind of real estate that Louis said could not be bought. Louis knew the value of real estate, for he owned two houses and a condo in Perris, the affordable suburb in the far-eastern reaches of the Inland Empire that he liked to call the *other* Paris. Even now Louis was doing his homework, watching a television show about increasing the resale value of houses with simple and inexpensive renovation ideas that involved thrift-store shopping, Dumpster diving, and attic treasure hunts.

"I love that stick-on floor tile they're using in the kitchen," Louis said. "From here, you can't even tell it's not really marble."

"Why don't you just live in one of those houses you bought?" Arthur said. Louis's apartment was even bleaker than before. With the inventory gone, the mismatched furniture was fully exposed, as were the walls, once white but now gray. "You should enjoy your quality of life. That's one thing I've learned this year."

"But I am enjoying my quality of life." Louis stretched out on the couch, from whose depths would later emerge a double-size bed for Arthur. "I'm thinking about how my renters pay my mortgage and how I'll profit from those houses in a few years. I'm thinking about how I'm going to corner the market in better than genuine goods, which is a bigger market than the one for things most people can't afford to buy."

This, Arthur realized, was the difference between them. Arthur thought of what he had done, what he was doing, or what he should have done, but Louis thought only of what he would do. For example, rather than resigning himself to saying "fake" or "knockoff," Louis preferred to say "better than genuine." But, he always emphasized, his wares actually were better, in the sense of being much, much cheaper. Why own one of the originals, he liked to say, when for the same price you could own a dozen, two dozen, even several dozen, of the better than genuine version?

"It's not all about money, Louis," Arthur said. "What about a wife? A family?"

"You mean love?" Louis pointed to the gold ring on Arthur's finger. "Can you say that's made you happy, Arthur?"

"It's not love's fault if things haven't worked out between me and Norma."

"I've tried love," Louis said, as if it were a kind of soft, malodorous French cheese. "It's okay, but the problem with it is the other person involved. She has a mind of her own. You can't say the same thing about things."

Arthur watched Louis for any sign of irony, but the small frown on Louis's face indicated he was serious. "Tell me about her," Arthur said. "Or was there more than one?"

"It's all in the past, Arthur." Louis gestured over his shoulder dismissively. "And I never think about the past. Every morning that I wake up I'm a new man."

Arthur had tried to get Louis to talk about himself before, never with any success, and so he changed the subject. "Thanks for letting me sleep over," Arthur said. "I appreciate it."

"You're my friend," Louis replied.

Arthur interpreted the statement to mean that he was Louis's only friend, for Louis never mentioned anyone else. "You're my friend, too," Arthur said, putting as much feeling as he could into his words. For a moment, the two of them maintained eye contact and smiled at each other. Then, before the situation became more emotionally complicated, Arthur excused himself to go take a shower.

The first inkling Arthur had the next morning of a less than auspicious day was the office computer crashing, taking with it into oblivion the last week's worth of record keeping. Despite Arthur's tinkering, the computer was still frozen at the end of the day, and it was a frustrated Arthur who climbed into his Chevy Nova, turned the ignition, and heard nothing but a mechanical screech, leaving him to ask for a jump start from Rubén, the Arellano & Sons landscaper who worked on Martín's house and who had once confessed to Arthur that he was *indocumentado*, which Arthur knew was true for more than one of Martín's gardeners. By the time Arthur stopped off at home to pick up fresh underwear and his razor before he went to Louis's, he was wondering what more could happen. Norma was in the kitchen, microwaving a TV dinner, and when she saw him, she gestured at the notepad by the phone, saying, "Someone called for you."

Arthur was relieved at having something to do besides scurrying furtively around his own home. The caller's name was Minh Vu, and as Arthur dialed the number, he wondered if this person was one of the many he had called months ago. While Arthur had not recognized the accents he had heard then as being of Vietnamese origin, he could now hear that accent quite clearly when Minh Vu answered the phone, even if his English was perfectly understandable as he said, "I think you know my father."

"I do?"

"His name is Men Vu."

"Oh, so you must be Louis's brother!" Arthur said. "He didn't tell me he had a brother named Minh."

During the brief pause on the phone, Arthur could hear a woman cooing to a crying child. Then Minh Vu said, "Who's Louis?"

The remaining conversation took six minutes. After Arthur hung up the phone with a shaking hand, he informed Norma that Men Vu had eight children, not four, none of whom was named Louis. One of them—Minh—had received the apology from the hospital after it had accidentally revealed their father's identity to the recipients of his organs. Seven strangers had inherited not just his liver but also his skin, his corneas, his ligaments, his pancreas, his lungs, and his heart, and these seven strangers now knew their father's name. For the past few months since the hospital's apology, the Vu clan had been arguing about whether or not to contact these seven strangers, and only now had they agreed to do so. At first, Arthur hadn't known whether to believe Louis or Minh Vu, who was outraged when Arthur said, "How do I know you are who you say you are?" But Arthur began to be convinced when, without hesitation, Minh Vu had provided him with a phone number, an address, and an invitation to visit his father's house in Stanton, where, he said, Arthur would find photographs, hospital records, X-rays, and ashes. Having kept himself calm for the time required to tell Norma the story, Arthur suddenly discovered himself in need of a drink. He found the last bottle of Wild Turkey he had ever bought stashed beneath the kitchen sink, half-full and untouched since the diagnosis.

"Oh, my God." The first sip brought tears to his eyes. "I can't believe this is happening."

"We've got to go over there, Art," Norma said, her dinner forgotten in the microwave. "Louis's got to tell us what's going on."

"No, this is up to me and him." The whiskey had burned off the fringes of his panic, and Arthur swallowed some more straight from the bottle. "Just the two of us."

"You are an idiot." Norma enunciated each word, as fierce as she was during the year of waiting. "What if he gets violent? We don't even know what he's capable of—he's been lying to us all this time. We don't know what he wants from us. We don't even know who he is."

But Arthur was not listening, the third shot of whiskey having run an electric wire from his throat to his gut and down to his toes, bringing him to his feet and out the door to the Chevy Nova despite Norma's entreaties. He was about to turn on the engine when the liver throbbed inside him, the size of a first-trimester fetus, forever expectant but never to be born, calling for his acknowledgment, gratitude, and love the way it constantly had done in the weeks after the operation, rendering him so breathless with its demand that he had to roll down the window and gasp for air. Overhead the moon was shining through a tear in a curtain of clouds, a perfect round bulb of white light reminding Arthur of the first thing he had seen upon awakening from his operation, a luminous orb floating in the darkness that he dimly understood to be heaven's beacon, telling him that he had crossed over to God's side. The orb grew steadily, its edges becoming hazy until it was a whiteness that filled his vision, a screen from behind which something metallic rattled and indistinct words were murmured. Someone was saying his name, a person, and not, as he had first thought, God, for Arthur was alive, a fact he knew both from the spear of pain thrust through his side, pinning his body to the bed, and from the voice he recognized as Norma's, calling him back to where he belonged.

w w w

On hearing of the conversation with Minh Vu from a breathless Arthur, Louis did not open the doors to any number of alternative futures and parallel universes where he was the son of the man who had saved Arthur's life. Instead, Louis merely sighed and shrugged. He was on his knees, sorting through a new shipment of goods, the boxes shoved up against the walls of the living room and labeled Donna Karan, Calvin Klein, and Vera Wang. While Arthur sank into the couch, Louis got up and raised his hands in a gesture of surrender. "I suppose it had to come out eventually, didn't it?" he said. "I'm sorry, Arthur. I didn't mean to hurt you."

Arthur closed his eyes and massaged his temples. In addition to the corkscrew of pain in his guts, a headache was chiseling out a groove in his skull. It made sense now why Louis had always been evasive about visiting Men Vu's grave. While Louis had attributed this to the bad blood that had run between him and his father, the real reason was that there was no blood at all.

"If you're not Louis Vu," said Arthur, "then who are you?"

"Who says I'm not Louis Vu?"

"You just made it up when I called you," Arthur said. "Louis Vuitton is your idol. And Vu is a very common Vietnamese name."

"Louis Vu is really my name," Louis said. "And I'm Chinese."

"Oh!" Arthur gasped. "I knew it! I knew you were Chinese!"

"But I was born in Vietnam, and I've never been to China." Louis sat down beside Arthur on the couch. "I can barely speak Chinese. So what does that make me? Chinese or Vietnamese? Both? Neither?"

"I don't know, and I don't care." Arthur groaned and rubbed his temples. "Why? Why did you do it?"

"Put yourself in my shoes, Arthur." Louis leaned back and crossed his legs, the feet capped in fake Fendi wingtips. "I get a phone call asking me if I am related to another man who shares my last name. Most people in my situation would say no. But I don't get your kind of phone call every day, and when I get it, I have to see where it takes me. So I played along. It's how I've gotten ahead."

"I want you to get your things out of my garage." The pressure in Arthur's head and the spike in his gut were ex-cruciating. "Tonight."

Louis shook his head mournfully. "I'm afraid not, Arthur."

"What do you mean, you're afraid not?"

"Don't get me wrong, Arthur. This is business, not per-sonal, okay? Otherwise, I like you a lot. We've had fun, haven't we? We're friends, aren't we?"

"We are not friends," Arthur said, his voice cracking because he really had considered Louis to be a friend.

"We're not friends?" Louis appeared genuinely hurt, his lower lip quivering. "Over something like this? Come on, Arthur!"

"Just get your things out of my garage tonight."

"But where would I put them?" Louis's lip stopped quivering, and an expression of gloom slowly descended on his face, dragging down the corners of his lips and eyebrows. "No, I'm afraid those things will have to stay. And please don't think of calling the cops. It might be hard to explain why you have a garage full of fake Miu Miu and Burberry."

"Then I'm going to take your things out of the garage myself," Arthur cried. "I'll take them out to the desert and leave them there."

"If I were you, Arthur, I'd think very carefully about touching my things."

"What are you going to do about it?"

"You've got something on me." Louis inspected his fingertips. "But I've got something on your brother, don't I?"

"What?"

"Come on, Arthur!" Louis's shout startled Arthur, who had never heard Louis raise his voice or seen him lean forward, as he did now, and snap his fingers an inch from Arthur's face. "Wake up! Who's your brother underpaying to clip his lawns and trim his hedges?"

The weight of Arthur's naïveté pressed him deeper into the couch as he recalled Rubén, Gustavo, Vicente, Alberto, and all those other employees of Arellano & Sons of whom his brother asked no questions, so long as they produced Social Security cards and driver's licenses, either real or faked well enough to be mistaken for real. Those phantom identities were easy to obtain, as Louis had shown Arthur one day, fanning out on the coffee table five driver's licenses, each one with Louis's picture but a different name. Arthur buried his face in his hands as he imagined a raid on Arellano & Sons, leading to arrests and deportations, with disgrace for Martín and defamation of Big Art's good name.

"I think it's time for you to go home, Arthur," Louis said, leaning back into his corner of the couch. His voice was tired, and his face was pale. "Why don't you just go home?"

The light in the bedroom was on when Arthur pulled into the driveway, although the rest of the house was dark. He was afraid of what Norma would say, so he bought some time by opening the garage door, in case the miracle he had prayed for on the drive home had actually happened. It hadn't. The boxes were still there, flaxen in the moonlight and stacked to the ceiling and the walls, right up to the edge of the drive-way. Louis had conquered every square foot of storage for his fountain pens with their plastic barrels, his sunglasses without ultraviolet protection, his watches that kept perfect time for a day, his designer jackets without linings, his pants with hems that unraveled easily, his discs of pirated movies filmed surreptitiously in theaters, his reproductions of Micro-soft software so perfect as to come with the bugs infesting the genuine item, his pseudopills that might or might not help, might or might not harm—a garage crammed with things fashioned by people whom he would never know but to whom

Arthur felt bound in some way, especially when he imagined the obscure places from where they might hail.

Greeting Arthur at eye level were the names of Gucci, Jimmy Choo, and Hedi Slimane, beautiful and exotic appellations written on the boxes with a blue marker. Arthur and Norma had yearned for such names upon encountering them in Bloomingdale's and window-shopping at the boutiques on Rodeo Drive, but when the clerks had ignored them, they understood that they themselves were unwanted.

"Arthur Arellano!"

Arthur turned. Norma stood at the back door in a frayed bathrobe, her feet bare. "I can explain," Arthur said, extending his arms hopefully. But when Norma folded her own arms over her chest and raised an eyebrow, he saw himself as she saw him then, offering nothing but empty hands.

I'D LOVE YOU TO WANT ME

*T*he first time the professor called Mrs. Khanh by the wrong name was at a wedding banquet, the kind of crowded affair they attended often, usually out of obligation. As the bride and groom approached their table, Mrs. Khanh noticed the professor reading his palms, where he'd jotted down his toast and the names of the newlyweds, whom they had never met. Leaning close to be heard over the chatter of four hundred guests and the din of the band, she found her husband redolent of well-worn paperbacks and threadbare carpet. It was a comforting mustiness, one that she associated with secondhand bookstores.

"Don't worry," she said. "You've done this a thousand times."

"Have I?" The professor rubbed his hands on his pants. "I can't seem to recall." His fair skin was thin as paper and lined with blue veins. From the precise part of his silver hair to the gleam on his brown oxfords, he appeared to be the same man who'd taught so many students he could no longer count them. During the two minutes the newlyweds visited their table, he didn't miss a beat, calling the couple by their correct names and bestowing the good wishes expected of him as the eldest among the ten guests. But while the groom tugged at the collar of his Nehru jacket and the bride plucked at the skirt of her empire-waist gown, Mrs. Khanh could think only of the night of the diagnosis, when the professor had frightened her by weeping for the first time in their four decades together. Only after the young couple left could she relax, sighing as deeply as she could in the strict confines of her velvet *ao dai*.

"The girl's mother tells me they're honeymooning for the first week in Paris." She spooned a lobster claw onto the professor's plate. "The second week they'll be on the French Riviera."

"Is that so?" Cracked lobster in tamarind sauce was Professor Khanh's favorite, but tonight he stared with doubt at the claw pointing toward him. "What did the French call Vung Tau?"

"Cap Saint Jacques."

"We had a very good time there. Didn't we?"

"That's when you finally started talking to me."

"Who wouldn't be shy around you," the professor murmured. Forty years ago, when she was nineteen and he was thirty-three, they had honeymooned at a beachside hotel on the cape. It was on their balcony, under a full, bright moon, listening to the French singing and shouting on their side of the beach, that the professor had suddenly started talking. "Imagine!" he said, voice filled with wonder as he began speaking about how the volume of the Pacific equaled the moon's. When he was finished, he went on to talk about the strange fish of deep sea canyons and then the inexplicability of rogue waves. If after a while she lost track of what he said, it hardly mattered, for by then the sound of his voice had seduced her, as reassuring in its measured tones as the first time she'd heard it, eavesdropping from her family's kitchen as he explained to her father his dissertation on the Kuroshio current's thermodynamics.

Now the professor's memories were gradually stealing away from him, and along with them the long sentences he once favored. When the band swung into "I'd Love You to Want Me," he loosened the fat Windsor knot of his tie and said, "Remember this song?"

"What about it?"

"We listened to it all the time. Before the children were born."

The song hadn't been released yet during her first pregnancy, but Mrs. Khanh said, "That's right."

"Let's dance." The professor leaned closer, draping one arm over the back of her chair. A fingerprint smudged one lens of his glasses. "You always insisted we dance when you heard this song, Yen."

"Oh?" Mrs. Khanh took a slow sip from her glass of water, hiding her surprise at being called by someone else's name. "When did we ever dance?"

The professor didn't answer, for the swelling chorus of the song had brought him to his feet. As he stepped toward the parquet dance floor, Mrs. Khanh seized the tail of his gray pinstripe jacket. "Stop it!" she said, pulling hard. "Sit down!"

Giving her a wounded look, the professor obeyed. Mrs. Khanh was aware of the other guests at their table staring at them. She held herself very still, unable to account for any woman named Yen. Perhaps Yen was an old acquaintance whom the professor never saw fit to mention, or the maternal grandmother whom Mrs. Khanh had never met and whose name she couldn't now recall, or a grade school teacher with whom he'd once been infatuated. Mrs. Khanh had begun preparing for many things, but she wasn't prepared for unknown people emerging from the professor's mind.

"The song's almost over," the professor said.

"We'll dance when we get home. I promise."

Despite his condition, or perhaps because of it, the professor insisted on driving them back. Mrs. Khanh was tense as she watched him handling the car, but he drove in his usual slow and cautious manner. He was quiet until he took a left at Golden West instead of a right, his wrong turn taking them by the community college from where he'd retired last spring. After coming to America, he'd been unable to find work in oceanography, and had settled for teaching Vietnamese. For

the last twenty years, he'd lectured under fluorescent light
ing to bored students. When Mrs. Khanh wondered if one of
those students might be Yen, she felt a jab of pain that she
mistook at first for heartburn. Only upon second thought did
she recognize it as jealousy.

The professor suddenly braked to a stop. Mrs. Khanh
braced herself with one hand against the dashboard and
waited to be called by that name again, but the professor made
no mention of Yen. He swung the car into a U-turn instead,
and as they headed toward home, he asked in a tone of great
reproach, "Why didn't you tell me we were going in the wrong
direction?" Watching all the traffic lights on the street ahead
of them turn green as if on cue, Mrs. Khanh realized that his
was a question for which she had no good answer.

The next morning, Mrs. Khanh was standing at the stove
preparing brunch for their eldest son's visit when the professor came into the kitchen, freshly bathed and shaved. He
took a seat at the kitchen counter, unfolded the newspaper,
and began reading to her from the headlines. Only after he'd
finished did she begin telling him about last night's events.
He'd asked her to inform him of those moments when he
no longer acted like himself, and she had gotten as far as
his lunge for the dance floor when the sag of his shoulders
stopped her.

"It's all right," she said, alarmed. "It's not your fault."

"But can you see me on the dance floor at my age?" The professor rolled up the newspaper and rapped it against the counter for emphasis. "And in my condition?"

Taking out a small blue notebook from his shirt pocket, the professor retreated to the patio, where he was writing down his errors when Vinh arrived. Fresh from his graveyard shift at the county hospital, their son wore a nurse's green scrubs, which, shapeless as they were, did little to hide his physique. If only he visited his parents as much as he did the gym, Mrs. Khanh thought. The edge of her hand could have fitted into the deep cleft of her son's chest, and her thighs weren't quite as thick as his biceps. Under one arm, he was carrying a bulky package wrapped in brown paper, which he propped against the trellis behind his father.

The professor slipped the notebook into his pocket and pointed his pen at the package. "What's the surprise?" he asked. While Mrs. Khanh brought out the eggs Benedict, Vinh stripped off the wrapping to reveal a painting in a heavy gilded frame evocative of nineteenth-century Europe. "It cost me a hundred dollars on Dong Khoi," he said. He had gone to Saigon on vacation last month. "The galleries there can knock off anything, but it was easier to frame it here."

The professor leaned forward to squint at the painting. "There was a time when that street was called Tu Do," he remarked wistfully. "And before that, Rue Catinat."

"I hoped you'd remember," Vinh said, sitting down next to his mother at the patio table. Mrs. Khanh could tell that the subject of the painting was a woman, but one whose left eye was green and whose right eye was red, which was nowhere near as odd as the way the artist had flattened her arms and torso, leaving her to look less like a real person and more like a child's paper doll, cut out and pasted to a three-dimensional chair. "There's a new study that shows how Picasso's paintings can stimulate people like Ba."

"Is that so?" The professor wiped his glasses with his napkin. Behind him was the scene to which Mrs. Khanh was now accustomed, an entrance ramp rising over their backyard and merging onto the freeway that Vinh would take home to Los Angeles, an hour north of their Westminster neighborhood. Her boys used to pass their afternoons spotting the makes and models of the passing cars, as if they were ornithologists distinguishing between juncos and sparrows. But that was a very long time ago, she thought, and Vinh was now a messenger dispatched by the rest of their six children.

"We think you should retire from the library, Ma," he said, knife and fork in hand. "We can send home enough money every month to cover all the bills. You can have a housekeeper to help you out. And a gardener, too."

Mrs. Khanh had never needed help with the garden, which was entirely of her own design. A horseshoe of green lawn divided a perimeter of persimmon trees from the center of the garden, where pale green cilantro, arrow-leafed basil, and Thai chilies grew abundantly in the beds she'd made for them. She seasoned her eggs Benedict with three dashes of pepper, and when she was certain that she could speak without betraying her irritation, she said, "I like to garden."

"Mexican gardeners come cheap, Ma. Besides, you'll want all the help you can get. You've got to be ready for the worst."

"We've seen much worse than you," the professor snapped. "We're ready for anything."

"And I'm not old enough for retirement," Mrs. Khanh added.

"Be reasonable." Vinh sounded nothing like the boy who, upon reaching his teenage years, had turned into someone his parents no longer knew, sneaking out of the house at night to be with his girlfriend, an American who painted her nails black and dyed her hair purple. The professor remedied the situation by nailing the windows shut, a problem Vinh solved by eloping soon after his graduation from Bolsa Grande High. "I'm in love," Vinh had screamed to his mother over the phone from Las Vegas. "But you wouldn't know anything about that, would you?" Sometimes Mrs. Khanh regretted ever telling him that her father had arranged her marriage.

"You don't need the money from that job," Vinh said. "But Ba needs you at home."

Mrs. Khanh pushed away her plate, the eggs barely touched. She wouldn't take advice from someone whose marriage hadn't lasted more than three years. "It's not about the money, Kevin."

Vinh sighed, for his mother used his American name only when she was upset with him. "Maybe you should help Ba," he said, pointing to the front of his father's polo shirt, marred by a splash of hollandaise sauce.

"Look at this," the professor said, brushing at the stain with his fingers. "It's only because you've upset me." Vinh sighed once more, but Mrs. Khanh refused to look at him as she dabbed a napkin in her glass of water. She wondered if he remembered their escape from Vung Tau on a rickety fishing trawler, overloaded with his five siblings and sixty strangers, three years after the war's end. After the fourth day at sea, he and the rest of the children, bleached by the sun, were crying for water, even though there was none to offer but the sea's. Nevertheless, she had washed their faces and combed their hair every morning, using salt water and spit. She was teaching them that decorum mattered even now, and that their mother's fear wasn't so strong that it could prevent her from loving them.

"Don't worry," she said. "The stain will come out." As she leaned forward to scrub the professor's shirt, Mrs. Khanh had a clear view of the painting. She liked neither the painting nor its gilded frame. It was too ornate for her taste, and seemed too old-fashioned for the painting. The disjuncture between the frame and the painting only exaggerated the painting's most disturbing feature, the way the woman's eyes looked forth from one side of her face. The sight of those eyes made Mrs. Khanh so uneasy that later that day, after Vinh went home, she moved the painting to the professor's library, where she left it facing a wall.

It wasn't long after their son's visit that the professor stopped attending Sunday mass. Mrs. Khanh stayed home as well, and gradually they began seeing less and less of their friends. The only times she left the house were to go shopping or to the Garden Grove library, where her fellow librarians knew nothing of the professor's illness. She enjoyed her part-time job, ordering and sorting the sizable collection of Vietnamese books and movies purchased for the residents of nearby Little Saigon, who, if they came to the library with a question, were directed to her perch behind the circulation desk. Answering those questions, Mrs. Khanh always felt the gratification that made her job worthwhile, the pleasure of being needed, if only for a brief amount of time.

When her shift ended at noon and she gathered her things to go home, she always did so with a sense of dread that shamed her. She made up for her shame by bidding good-bye to the other librarians with extra cheer, and by preparing the house for emergencies with great energy, as if she could forestall the inevitable through hard work. She marked a path from bed to bathroom with fluorescent yellow tape, so the professor wouldn't get lost at night, and on the wall across from the toilet, she taped a sign at eye level that said FLUSH. She composed a series of lists which, posted strategically around the house, reminded the professor in what order to put his clothes on, what to put in his pockets before he left home, and what times of the day he should eat. But it was the professor who hired a handyman to install iron bars on the windows. "You wouldn't want me sneaking out at night," the professor said with resignation, leaning his forehead against the bars. "And neither would I."

For Mrs. Khanh, the more urgent problem was the professor coming home as a stranger. Whereas her husband was never one to be romantic, this stranger returned from one of the afternoon walks he insisted on taking by himself with a red rose in a plastic tube. He'd never before bought flowers of any sort, preferring to surprise her with more enduring presents, like the books he gave her every now and again, on topics like how to make friends and influence people, or income tax preparation. Once he had surprised her by giving her fiction, a collection of short stories by an author she had never heard of before. Even this effort was slightly off the mark, for she preferred novels. She never read past the title pages of his gifts, satisfied at seeing her name penned in his elegant hand beneath those of the authors. But if the professor had spent his life practicing calligraphy, he'd never given a thought to presenting roses, and when he bowed while offering her the flower, he appeared to be suffering from a stomach cramp.

"Who's this for?" she asked.

"Is there anyone else here?" The professor shook the rose for emphasis, and one of its petals, browning at the edges, fell off. "It's for you."

"It's very pretty." She took the rose reluctantly. "Where did you get it?"

"Mr. Esteban. He tried selling me oranges also, but I said we had our own."

"And who am I?" she demanded. "What's my name?"

He squinted at her. "Yen, of course."

"Of course." Biting her lip, she fought the urge to snap the head off the rose. She displayed the flower in a vase on the dining table for the professor's sake, but by the time she brought out dinner an hour later, he had forgotten he bought it. As he nibbled on blackened tiger shrimp, grilled on skewers, and tofu shimmering in black bean sauce, he talked animatedly instead about the postcard they'd received that afternoon from their eldest daughter, working for American Express in Munich. Mrs. Khanh examined the picture of the Marienplatz before turning over the postcard to read aloud the note, which remarked on the curious absence of pigeons.

"Little things stay with you when you travel," observed the professor, sniffing at the third course, a soup of bitter melon. Their children had never acquired the taste for it, but it reminded the professor and Mrs. Khanh of their own childhood.

"Such as?"

"The price of cigarettes," the professor said. "When I returned to Saigon after finishing my studies, I couldn't buy my daily Gauloises any longer. The imported price was too much."

She leaned the postcard against the vase, where it would serve as a memento of the plans they'd once made for traveling to all of the world's great cities after their retirement. The only form of transport Mrs. Khanh had ruled out was the ocean cruise. Open expanses of water prompted fears of drowning, a phobia so strong that she no longer took baths, and even when showering kept her back to the spray.

"Now why did you buy that?" the professor asked.

"The postcard?"

"No, the rose."

"I didn't buy it." Mrs. Khanh chose her words carefully, not wanting to disturb the professor too much, and yet wanting him to know what he had done. "You did."

"Me?" The professor was astonished. "Are you certain?"

"I am absolutely certain," she said, surprised to hear the gratification in her voice.

The professor didn't notice. He only sighed and took out the blue notebook from the pocket of his shirt. "Let's hope that won't happen again," he muttered.

"I don't suppose it will." Mrs. Khanh stood to gather the dishes. She hoped her face didn't show her anger, convinced as she was that the professor had intended the rose for this other woman. She was carrying four plates, the tureen, and both their glasses when, at the kitchen's threshold, the wobbling weight of her load became too much. The sound of silverware clattering on the tiled floor and the smash of porcelain breaking made the professor cry out from the dining room. "What's that?" he shouted.

Mrs. Khanh stared at the remains of the tureen at her feet. Three uneaten green coins of bitter melon, stuffed with pork, lay sodden on the floor among the shards. "It's nothing," she said. "I'll take care of it."

After he'd fallen asleep later that evening, she went to his library, where the painting she had propped by his desk was now turned face forward. She sighed. If he kept turning the painting this way, she would at least have to reframe it in something more modern and suitable. She sat down at his desk, flanked on either side by bookshelves that held several hundred volumes in Vietnamese, French, and English. His ambition was to own more books than he could ever possibly read, a desire fueled by having left behind all his books when they had fled Vietnam. Dozens of paperbacks cluttered his desk, and she had to shove them aside to find the notebooks where he'd been tracking his mistakes over the past months. He had poured salt into his coffee and sprinkled sugar into his soup; when a telemarketer had called, he'd agreed to five-year subscriptions to *Guns & Ammo* and *Cosmopolitan*; and one day he'd tucked his wallet in the freezer, giving new meaning to the phrase cold, hard cash, or so he'd joked with her when she discovered it. But there was no mention of Yen, and after a moment's hesitation, underneath his most recent entry, Mrs. Khanh composed the following: "Today I called my wife by the name of Yen," she wrote. She imitated the flourishes of the professor's penmanship with great care, pretending that what she was doing was for the professor's own good. "This mistake must not be repeated."

The following morning, the professor held forth his coffee cup and said, "Please pass me the sugar, Yen." The next day, as she trimmed his hair in the bathroom, he asked, "What's on television tonight, Yen?" As he called her by the other woman's name again and again over the following weeks, the question of who this woman was consumed her days. Perhaps Yen was a childhood crush, or a fellow student of his graduate school years in Marseille, or even a second wife in Saigon, someone he'd visited on the way home from the university, during those long early evening hours when he told her he was sitting in his office on campus, correcting student exams. She recorded every incident of mistaken identity in his notebooks, but the next morning he would read her forgeries without reaction, and not long afterward would call her Yen once more, until she thought she might burst into tears if she heard that name again.

The woman was most likely a fantasy found by the professor's wandering mind, or so she told herself after catching him naked from the waist down, kneeling over the bathtub and scrubbing furiously at his pants and underwear under a jet of hot water. Glaring over his shoulder, the professor had screamed, "Get out!" She jumped back, slamming the bathroom door in her haste. Never before had the professor lost such control of himself, or yelled at her, not even in those first days after coming to southern California, when they'd eaten from food stamps, gotten housing assistance, and worn secondhand clothes donated by the parishioners of St. Albans. That was true love, she thought, not giving roses but going to work every day and never once complaining about teaching Vietnamese to so-called heritage learners, immigrant and refugee students who already knew the language but merely wanted an easy grade.

Not even during the most frightening time of her life, when they were lost on the great azure plain of the sea, rolling unbroken to the horizon, did the professor raise his voice. By the fifth evening, the only sounds besides the waves slapping at the hull were children whimpering and adults praying to God, Buddha, and their ancestors. The professor hadn't prayed. Instead, he had stood at the ship's bow as if he were at his lectern, the children huddled together at his knees for protection against the evening wind, and told them lies. "You can't see it even in daylight," he'd said, "but the current we're traveling on is going straight to the Philippines, the way it's done since the dawn of time." He repeated his story so often even she allowed herself to believe it, until the afternoon of the seventh day, when they saw, in the distance, the rocky landing strip of a foreign coast. Nesting upon it were the huts of a fishing village, seemingly composed of twigs and grass, brooded over by a fringe of mangroves. At the sight of land, she had thrown herself into the professor's arms, knocking his glasses askew, and sobbed openly for the first time in front of her startled children. She was so seized by the ecstasy of knowing that they would all live that she had blurted out "I love you." It was something she had never said in public and hardly ever in private, and the professor, embarrassed by their children's giggles, had only smiled and adjusted his glasses. His embarrassment only deepened once they reached land, which the locals informed them was the north shore of eastern Malaysia.

For some reason, the professor never spoke of this time at sea, although he referred to so many other things they had done in the past together, including events of which she had no recollection. The more she listened to him, the more she feared her own memory was faltering. Perhaps they really had eaten ice cream flavored with durian on the veranda of a tea plantation in the central highlands, reclining on rattan chairs. And was it possible they'd fed bamboo shoots to the tame deer in the Saigon zoo? Or together had beaten off a pickpocket, a scabby refugee from the bombed-out country-side who'd sneaked up on them in the Ben Thanh market?

As the days of spring lengthened into summer, she answered the phone less and less, eventually turning off the ringer so the professor wouldn't answer calls either. She was afraid that if someone asked for her, he would say, "Who?" Even more worrying was the prospect of him speaking to their friends or children of Yen. When her daughter phoned from Munich, she said, "Your father's not doing so well," but left the details vague. She was more forthcoming with Vinh, knowing that whatever she told him he would e-mail to the other children. Whenever he left a message, she could hear the hiss of grease in a pan, or the chatter of a news channel, or the beeping of horns. He called her on his cell phone only as he did something else. She admitted that as much as she loved her son, she liked him very little, a confession that made her unhappy with herself until the day she called him back and he asked, "Have you decided? Are you going to quit?"

"Don't make me tell you one more time." She wrapped the telephone cord tightly around her index finger. "I'm never going to quit."

After she hung up the phone, she returned to the task of changing the sheets the professor had bed-wet the previous evening. Her head was aching from lack of sleep, her back was sore from the chores, and her neck was tight with worry. When bedtime came, she was unable to sleep, listening to the professor talk about how gusts of the mistral blew him from one side to the other of the winding narrow streets of Le Panier, where he'd lived in a basement apartment during his Marseille years, or about the hypnotic sound made by the scratch of a hundred pens on paper as students took their exams. As he talked, she studied the dim light in their bedroom, cast off from the streetlamps outside, and remembered how the moon over the South China Sea was so bright that even at midnight she could see the fearful expressions on her children's faces. She was counting the cars passing by outside, listening for the sounds of their engines and hoping for sleep, when the professor touched her hand in the dark. "If you close your eyes," he said gently, "you might hear the ocean."

Mrs. Khanh closed her eyes.

September came and went. October passed and the Santa Ana winds came, rushing from the mountains to the east with the force of freeway traffic, breaking the stalks of the Egyptian papyruses she'd planted in ceramic pots next to the trellis. She no longer allowed the professor to walk by himself in the afternoons, but instead followed him discreetly at a distance of ten or twenty feet, clutching her hat against the winds. If the

Santa Ana had subsided, they read together on the patio. Over the past few months, the professor had taken to reading out loud, and slowly. Each day he seemed to read even more loudly, and more slowly, until the afternoon in November when he stopped in mid-sentence for so long that the silence shook Mrs. Khanh from the grip of Quynh Dao's latest romance.

"What's the matter?" she asked, closing her book.

"I've been trying to read this sentence for five minutes," the professor said, staring at the page. When he looked up, she saw tears in his eyes. "I'm losing my mind, aren't I?"

From then on, she read to him whenever she was free, from books on academic topics she had no interest in whatsoever. She stopped whenever he began reciting a memory—the anxiety he felt on meeting her father for the first time, while she waited in the kitchen to be introduced; the day of their wedding, when he nearly fainted from the heat and the tightness of his cravat; or the day they returned to Saigon three years ago and visited their old house on Phan Than Gian, which they could not find at first because the street had been renamed Dien Bien Phu. Saigon had also changed names after it changed hands, but they couldn't bring themselves to call it Ho Chi Minh City. Neither could the taxi driver who ferried them from their hotel to the house, even though he was too young to remember a time when the city was officially Saigon.

They parked two houses down from their old house, and stayed in the taxi to avoid the revolutionary cadres from the north who had moved in after the Communist takeover. She and the professor were nearly overwhelmed by sadness and rage, fuming as they wondered who these strangers were who had taken such poor care of their house. The solitary alley lamp illuminated tears of rust streaking the walls, washed down from the iron grill of the terrace by the monsoon rain. As the taxi's wipers squeaked against the windshield, a late-night masseur biked past, announcing his calling with the shake of a glass bottle filled with pebbles.

"You told me it was the loneliest sound in the world," said the professor.

Before he started talking, she'd been reading to him from a biography of de Gaulle, and her finger was still on the last word she'd read. She didn't like to think about their lost home, and she didn't remember having said any such thing. "The wipers or the glass bottle?" she asked.

"The bottle."

"It seemed so at the time," she lied. "I hadn't heard that sound in years."

"We heard it often. In Dalat." The professor took off his glasses and wiped them with his handkerchief. He had gone once to a resort in the mountains of Dalat for a conference while she stayed in Saigon, pregnant. "You always wanted to eat your ice cream outside in the evenings," the professor continued. "But it's hard to eat ice cream in the tropics, Yen. One has no time to savor it. Unless one is indoors, with air conditioning."

"Dairy products give you indigestion."

"If one eats ice cream in a bowl, it rapidly becomes soup. If one eats it in a cone, it melts all over one's hand." When he turned to her and smiled, she saw gumdrops of mucus in the corners of his eyes. "You loved those brown sugar cones, Yen. You insisted that I hold yours for you so your hand wouldn't get sticky."

A breeze rattled the bougainvillea, the first hint, perhaps, of the Santa Ana returning. The sound of her own voice shocked her as well as the professor, who stared at her with his mouth agape when she said, "That's not my name. I am not that woman, whoever she is, if she even exists."

"Oh?" The professor slowly closed his mouth and put his glasses back on. "Your name isn't Yen?"

"No," she said.

"Then what is it?"

She wasn't prepared for the question, having been worried only about her husband calling her by the wrong name. They rarely used each other's proper names, preferring endearments like *Anh*, for him, or *Em*, for her, and when they spoke to each other in front of the children, they called themselves Ba and Ma. Usually she heard her first name spoken only by friends, relatives, or bureaucrats, or when she introduced herself to someone new, as she was, in a sense, doing now.

"My name is Sa," she said. "I am your wife."

"Right." The professor licked his lips and took out his notebook.

That evening, after they had gone to bed and she heard him breathing evenly, she switched on her lamp and reached across his body for the notebook, propped on the alarm clock.

His writing had faded into such a scribble that she was forced to read what he wrote twice, following the jags and peaks of his letters down a dog-eared page until she reached the bottom, where she deciphered the following: *Matters worsening. Today she insisted I call her by another name. Must keep closer eye on her*—here she licked her finger and used it to turn the page—*for she may not know who she is anymore.* She closed the book abruptly, with a slap of the pages, but the professor, curled up on his side, remained still. A scent of sweat and sulfur emanated from underneath the sheets. If it wasn't for his quiet breathing and the heat of his body, he might have been dead, and for a moment as fleeting as déjà vu, she wished he really were.

In the end there was no choice. On her last day at work, her fellow librarians threw her a surprise farewell party, complete with cake and a wrapped gift box that held a set of travel guides for the vacations they knew she'd always wanted to take. She fondled the guides for a while, riffling through their pages, and when she almost wept, her fellow librarians thought she was being sentimental. Driving home with the box of guides in the backseat, next to a package of adult diapers she'd picked up from Sav-On's that morning, she fought to control the sense that ever so slowly the book of her life was being closed.

When she opened the door to their house and called out his name, she heard only bubbling from the fish tank. After not finding him in any of the bedrooms or bathrooms, she left the diapers and box of books in his library. An open copy of *Sports Illustrated* was on his recliner in the living room, a half-eaten jar of applesauce sat on the kitchen counter, and in the backyard, the chenille throw he wore around his lap in cool weather lay on the ground. Floating in his teacup on the patio table was a curled petal from the bougainvillea, shuttling back and forth.

Panic almost made her call the police. But they wouldn't do anything so soon; they'd tell her to call back when he was missing for a day or two. As for Vinh, she ruled him out, not wanting to hear him say, "I told you so." Regret swept over her then, a wave of feeling born from her guilt over being so selfish. Her librarian's instinct for problem solving and orderly research kept her standing under the weight of that regret, and she returned to her car determined to find the professor. She drove around her block first before expanding in ever-widening circles, the windows rolled down on both sides. The neighborhood park, where she and the professor often strolled, was abandoned except for squirrels chasing each other through the branches of an oak tree. The sidewalks were empty of pedestrians or joggers, except for a withered man in a plaid shirt standing on a corner, selling roses from plastic buckets and oranges from crates, his eyes shaded by a grimy baseball cap. When she called him Mr. Esteban, his eyes widened; when she asked him if he'd seen the professor, he smiled apologetically and said, "No hablo inglés. Lo siento."

Doubling back on her tracks, she drove each street and lane and cul-de-sac a second time. Leaning out the window, she called his name, first in a low voice, shy about making a scene, and then in a shout. "Anh Khanh!" she cried. "Anh Khanh!" A few window curtains twitched, and a couple of passing cars slowed down, their drivers glancing at her curiously. But he didn't spring forth from behind anyone's hedges, or emerge from a stranger's door.

Only after it was dark did she return. The moment she walked through the front door, she smelled the gas. A kettle was on the stove, but the burner hadn't been lit. Both her pace and her pulse quickened from a walk to a sprint. After shutting off the gas, she saw that the glass doors leading to the patio, which she'd closed before her departure, were slightly ajar. There was a heavy, long flashlight in one of the kitchen drawers, and the heft of the aluminum barrel in her hand was comforting as she slowly approached the glass doors. But when she shone the light over the patio and onto the garden, she saw only her persimmon trees and the red glint of the chilies.

She was in the hallway when she saw the light spilling out of the professor's library. When she peeked around the door frame, she saw the professor with his back to the door. At his feet was her box of books, and he stood facing the bookshelf that was reserved for her. Here, she kept her magazines and the books he'd given her over the years. The professor knelt, picked a book from the box, and stood up to shelve it. He repeated the same motion, one book at a time. *Hidden Tahiti and French Polynesia.* Frommer's *Hawaii. National Geographic Traveler: The Caribbean.* With each book, he mumbled something she couldn't hear, as if he might be trying to read the titles on the spines. *Essential Greek Islands. Jerusalem and the Holy Land. World Cultures: Japan. A Romantic's Guide to Italy.* He touched the cover of each book with great care, tenderly, and she knew, not for the first time, that it wasn't she who was the love of his life.

The professor shelved the last book and turned around. The expression on his face when he saw her was the one he'd worn forty years ago at their first meeting, when she'd entered the living room of her father's house and seen him pale with anxiety, eyes blinking in anticipation. "Who are you?" he cried, raising his hand as if to ward off a blow. Her heart was beating fast and her breathing was heavy. When she swallowed, her mouth was dry, but she could feel a sheen of dampness on her palms. It struck her then that these were the same sensations she'd felt that first time, seeing him in a white linen suit wrinkled by high humidity, straw fedora pinned between hand and thigh.

"It's just me," she said. "It's Yen."

"Oh," the professor said, lowering his hand. He sat down heavily in his armchair, and she saw that his oxfords were encrusted in mud. As she crossed the carpet to the bookshelf, he followed her with a hooded gaze, his look one of exhaustion. She was about to take *Les Petites Rues de Paris* from the bookshelf for the evening's reading, but when she saw him close his eyes and lean back in his armchair, it was clear that he wouldn't be traveling anywhere. Neither would she. Having ruled out the travel guides, she decided against the self-help books and the how-to manuals as well. Then she saw the thin and uncracked spine of the book of short stories.

A short story, she thought, would be just long enough.

Sitting beside him on the carpet, she found herself next to the painting. She turned her back to the woman with the two eyes on one side of her face, and she promised herself that tomorrow she would have the painting reframed. When she opened the book, she could feel the woman looking over her shoulder at her name, written in his precise hand under that of the author. She wondered what, if anything, she knew about love. Not much, perhaps, but enough to know that what she would do for him now she would do again tomorrow, and the next day, and the day after that. She would read out loud, from the beginning. She would read with measured breath, to the very end. She would read as if every letter counted, page by page and word by word.

THE AMERICANS

*I*f it weren't for his daughter and his wife, James Carver would never have ventured into Vietnam, a country about which he knew next to nothing except what it looked like at forty thousand feet. But Michiko had insisted on visiting after Claire invited them, her e-mail addressed to *Mom and Dad* but really meant for her mother. Michiko was the one who wanted to see Vietnam, hearing from relatives who had toured there that it reminded them of Japan's bucolic past, before General MacArthur wielded the postwar hand of reconstruction to daub Western makeup on Japanese features. Carver, however, cared little for pastoral fantasies, having passed his childhood in a rural Alabama hamlet siphoned clean of hope long before his birth. He had refused to go until Michiko compromised, proposing Angkor Wat as the prelude and Thailand's beaches and temples as the postscript to a brief Vietnamese sojourn.

This was how Carver found himself in September in Hue, walking slowly through the grounds of an imperial tomb with Michiko, Claire, and her boyfriend, Khoi Legaspi. Legaspi's optimism and serenity irked Carver, as did the poor fit between Legaspi's Asian appearance and his surname, bestowed on him by his adoptive parents. The young man, perhaps sensing this ambivalence, had been solicitous of him throughout his visit, but Carver found Legaspi's attention patronizing rather than helpful.

Before they embarked on their tour through the imperial tombs this morning, for example, Legaspi had attempted to sympathize with Carver by mentioning how his own father was forced to walk with a cane. "That's worse than your situation," Legaspi said. The comment irritated Carver, implying as it did that he was somehow whining about having broken his hip three years ago, when he had fallen down the stairway of his own house. Now he was sixty-eight and limping, determined not to be outpaced by Legaspi as he led them through the grounds of the tomb, which more closely resembled a summer palace, its pavilion overlooking a moat filled with lotuses.

"I might go back and finish my doctorate," Legaspi said in response to a question from Michiko. Fit and slender in khakis and a burnt orange polo shirt, he resembled the college students at Bowdoin whom Carver saw loitering on the sidewalks whenever he drove to town. "But maybe not. I suppose after a while the pure research was not enough. I wanted to apply the research."

"I'd love to see your robot in action." Michiko brushed her hand against the mossy flank of a millennium-old wall, varnished black by the centuries. The royal past alluded to was nowhere near as grand as Buckingham Palace or Versailles, which Carver had seen during layovers on the European routes he had piloted for Pan Am, but the tomb had its own melancholic charm. "And the mongoose."

"How about the day after tomorrow?" Legaspi said. "I can set up a demonstration."

"What do you think, Dad?" Carver saw once again the crow's-feet around Claire's eyes, newly engraved since her departure for Vietnam two years ago. She was only twenty-six. "It'll be educational."

"Angkor Wat was pretty educational." Carver didn't like being educated on his vacations. "And we visited that terrible war museum in Saigon. I don't really feel like seeing any more horrors."

"What you'll see is the future of demining," Claire said. "Not people crawling on their knees digging out mines by hand."

"Won't this robot put those people out of work?"

"That is not the kind of work people should do," Legaspi said. "Robots were invented to free people from danger and slavery."

Carver's ears twitched. "You said the Department of Defense was funding your adviser's research at MIT. Why exactly do you think the DOD is interested in these robots?"

"Dad," Claire said.

"We have to take the money where we find it." Legaspi shrugged. "The world isn't a pure place."

"Famous last words."

"Jimmy," said Michiko.

"All I'm saying is not to underestimate the military-industrial complex."

"I suppose you'd know," Claire said.

"How about a picture?" Legaspi proposed. Carver groaned silently. He hated taking pictures, but Michiko loved commemorating every occasion, important or trivial. For her sake, he took his place obediently between his wife and daughter, who themselves were flanked by two gray stone mandarins, goateed and with swords on their shoulders. They were shorter even than Michiko and Claire, and Carver assumed they were life-size from the time of this emperor whose name he suddenly could not recall as Legaspi aimed the camera. It was true that this was the third tomb they were visiting on the Perfume River, but it still bothered Carver that he could not remember this emperor's name, which Legaspi had mentioned several times.

Becoming stupider was a consequence of age for which he was unprepared. With age was supposed to come wisdom, but he wasn't certain what wisdom felt like, whereas intelligence he knew to be a constant firing of the synapses, the brain a six-barreled Gatling gun of activity. Now his mind was shooting thoughts through only one or two barrels. He hadn't been this slow since Claire and William were newborns, their nighttime neediness calling him from his sleep. Now his son

was twenty-eight, and Carver dated the beginning of his decline to William's graduation from the Air Force Academy
six years ago, one of the proudest moments in Carver's life.
William had also become a pilot, but he was unhappy flying
a KC-135, refueling bombers and fighters patrolling the skies
of Iraq and Afghanistan. "It's boring, Dad," William had said
over the phone during their last conversation. "I'm a truck
driver."

"Truck driving is good," Carver said. "Truck driving is
honorable."

Most important, flying a tanker was safe, unlike Carver's
own job during his military years when he piloted a B-52, an
ungainly blue whale of a plane that he loved with an intensity still felt as a lingering hunger. During different tours in
the late sixties and early seventies, he launched from Guam,
Okinawa, and Thailand, never finding himself freer than in
the cockpit's tight squeeze, entrusted with a majestic machine
carrying within its womb thirty tons of iron bombs, and yet for
all that vulnerable as a Greek demigod. Two bombers of his
wing had collided with each other over the South China Sea,
the bodies of the crews lost forever, while another B-52 in his
cell was transformed into a flaming cross as it fell in the night
sky, tail clipped by a surface-to-air missile, the two survivors
spending the next four years in the Hanoi Hilton. Better to be
safe, Carver wanted to tell William, but he refrained. William
would hear the lie. As an airman, William knew that if his
father could live life all over again, Carver wouldn't hesitate
to crawl once more through the narrow breech in the paunch

of the B-52's fuselage, the entry never failing to make him quiver with anticipation.

The next morning Claire hired a van to take her parents on the two-hour ride to Quang Tri, where she was living and where Legaspi's demining operation was based. When Claire showed them her studio apartment, Carver was relieved to see only a twin-sized bed, shrouded behind a mosquito net. A window and narrow horizontal slits at the top of the high walls provided ventilation, the air pushed about by a ceiling fan that rotated as slowly as a chicken on a spit. The kitchen consisted of a heat-scarred, two-burner portable gas stove on a countertop with black veins in the grouting, while the bathroom had no separate shower stall, only a drain in the floor next to the toilet, the showerhead on a hose. Posters of rock bands—Dengue Fever, Death Cab for Cutie, Hot Hot Heat—papered the walls above the cinder blocks and wood boards where Claire shelved her clothing.

"Couldn't you find a better place, dear?" Michiko fanned herself with her sun hat. "You don't even have an air conditioner."

"This is better than what most people have. Even if people could afford this place, there'd be an entire family in here."

"You're not a native," Carver said. "You're an American."

"That's a problem I'm trying to correct."

Recalling a lesson from the couples therapy Michiko had persuaded him to attend, Carver counted down from ten.

Claire watched with her arms crossed, face as impassive as it was when he spanked her in her childhood, or shouted at her in the teenage years when she repeatedly crossed whatever line he'd drawn.

"Enough, you two," Michiko said. "People are always a little cranky without their coffee, aren't they?"

Claire's apartment was situated above a café. Carver sipped black coffee on ice at their sidewalk table, squatting on a plastic stool and watching Michiko spend five dollars buying postcards and lighters from four barefoot children, dark as dust, who bounded up the moment they sat down. After their sales, the quartet retreated a few feet and stood with their backs to a row of parked motorbikes, giggling and staring.

"Haven't they seen tourists before?" Carver said.

"Not like us." Claire unsealed a pack of cigarettes and lit one. "We're a mixed bag."

"They don't know what to make of us?" Michiko said. "I'm used to it, but you're not."

"Try being a Japanese wife at a Michigan air base in 1973."

"Touché," Claire said.

"Try being a black man in Japan," Carver said. "Or Thailand."

"But you could always go home," Claire said. "There was always a place for you somewhere. But there's never been a place for me."

She said it matter-of-factly, without any of the melodrama of her adolescence, when she would come home from school sobbing at a slight from a peer or a stranger, some variation along the line of *What are you?* Her tears agonized Carver, making him feel guilty for delivering her into a world determined to put everybody in her proper place. He wanted to find the culprit who had hurt his daughter and beat some sense into the kid's head, but he restrained himself, as he had whenever he encountered the look in people's eyes that said *What are you doing here?* In the one-room library of the small town five miles down the road from his hamlet; at Penn State, which he attended on an ROTC scholarship; in flight school at Randolph Air Force Base; in an airman's uniform; in his B-52 and later his Boeing airliner, he was never where he was supposed to be. He had survived by focusing on his goal, ascending ever higher, refusing to see the sneers and doubt in his peripheral vision.

But now retired, limping out of his sixties, he no longer knew what his goal should be. He envied Claire her sense of mission, teaching English to people as poor as the dirt farmers and sharecroppers of his childhood, their skin as brown and cracked as the soil they tilled, the desiccated earth of summer's oppressive months. She exhibited a confidence that pleased him as he watched her hail a taxi, give directions in Vietnamese to the English school, and greet the students clustered in the courtyard under the shade of flame trees. When Claire gestured at Carver and Michiko and said something in the local language, the students greeted them in pitch-perfect English. "Hello!" "How are you!" "Good morning, Mr. and Mrs. Carver!" Carver smiled at them and waved back. Smiling at your relatives never got you very far, but smiling at strangers and acquaintances sometimes did.

A few doors down the colonnade from the courtyard was Claire's classroom, her wooden desk confronting several rows of short tables and benches. Acne scars of white plaster were visible, the yellow paint of the walls having peeled away in a multitude of places. On the blackboard behind the desk, someone—it must have been Claire herself—had written "The Passive Voice" in big, bold letters. Underneath was written "my bicycle was stolen" and "mistakes were made."

"How many students do you have, dear?" Michiko said.

"Four classes of thirty each."

"That's too much," Carver said. "You're not paid enough to do that."

"They really want to learn. And I really want to teach."

"So you've been here two years." Carver toed a slab of tile flaking loose from the floor. "How much longer are you planning to stay?"

"Indefinitely."

"What do you mean, indefinitely?"

"I like it here, Dad."

"You like it here," Carver said. "Look at this place."

Claire deliberately swept her gaze over her classroom. "I'm looking."

"What your father means is that we want you back home because we love you."

"That's what I mean."

"I am home, Mom. It sounds strange, I don't know how to put it, but I feel like this is where I'm supposed to be. I have a Vietnamese soul."

"That's the stupidest thing I've ever heard," Carver shouted.

"It's not stupid," Claire hissed. "Don't say that. You always say that."

"Name three times I've said that."

"When I left Maine for school." Claire held up three fingers of her right hand and slowly curled each one into her palm as she counted the times, ending up with a balled fist. "When I majored in women's studies. When I told you I was going to Vietnam to teach. And those are just the most recent ones to come to mind."

"But those things *are* stupid."

"Oh, God, God, God." Claire beat her fist on her forehead. "Why do I ever think things will be different with you?"

"For Chrissakes," Carver muttered. Whispering drew his attention to the door, where a handful of the students had clustered. Claire wiped tears from her eyes. "Look! Now you've made me lose face with them."

"Lose face?" Carver said. "You really do think you're turning into one of them."

"Shut up, James." Michiko pushed by him to offer Claire a tissue. "I think we've had just about enough family time together, don't you?"

While Claire escorted Michiko on a shopping expedition for local textiles, Carver was forced to entertain himself,

a problem since there was nothing to recommend Quang Tri
to the foreign visitor except its proximity to the old Demilita-
rized Zone. The city was just a provincial town that had been
destroyed in the course of the war and, from all reports, there
had not been that much to see before its destruction. Carver
passed the time sitting at a bar's sidewalk patio and watching
local boys play soccer on a patch of grass. By the time the monsoon arrived in the afternoon, he had drunk enough 33 Beer to
remind himself that nothing had changed since he had drunk
it in Thailand over thirty years ago. If you're going to bomb
a country, his roommate in U-Tapao had said, you should at
least drink its beer. It was insipid then and it was insipid now.
As curtains of rain swept over the road, he ordered a bottle of
Hue instead. Watching the water flooding through the gutters,
Carver longed for his clapboard cottage on the shore of Basin
Cove, autumn waving its metamorphosing wand over the for-
est's greenery. That new world of crimson and gold receded
even further when the lady who ran the market next to the
bar turned up the volume of her radio. Above the relentless
hammering of the rain, a woman's high-pitched voice whined
in accompaniment with what sounded like a xylophone, the
music pregnant with sorrow, although perhaps it was only
Carver who heard a lamentation where there was none.

The demining site was half an hour from their hotel in Quang
Tri the next afternoon, far beyond the outskirts of the city.
Legaspi had promised to pick them up in a white buffalo, and

when Carver had asked him if he really meant a white buffalo, Legaspi had winked and said, "You'll see." The white buffalo turned out to be a white Toyota Land Cruiser speckled with measles of rust, its counter reading over 300,000 kilometers.

"Locals call these things white buffalo because they're as plentiful as white buffalo," Legaspi said from the driver's seat. "The foreigners and the NGOs and the UN love the Land Cruiser."

"Donor money," Carver said. "All the doughnuts and four-wheel drives you can buy."

"Pretty much, Mr. Carver."

Michiko and Claire sat in the backseat, Carver in the front. Lining the road outside Quang Tri were one- and two-story homes of faded wood and corrugated tin, a few freshly painted and plastered mini-mansions towering over their primitive neighbors, all of them long and narrow. Occasionally a cemetery or a temple came into view, encrusted with dragonesque architectural filigree, as well as a couple of churches, their ascetic walls plain and whitewashed.

The flat fields behind the homes were mostly devoid of trees and shade, some of the plots growing rice and the others devoted to crops Carver did not recognize, their color the dull, muted green of an algae bloom, the countryside nowhere near as lush and verdant as the Thai landscape visible from Carver's cockpit window as his B-52 ascended over the waters of Thale Sap Songkhla, destined for the enemy cities of the north or the Plain of Jars. There was a reason he loved flying. Almost everything looked more beautiful from a distance, the earth becoming ever more perfect as one ascended and came closer to seeing the world from God's eyes, man's hovels and palaces disappearing, the peaks and valleys of geography fading to become strokes of a paintbrush on a divine sphere. But seen up close, from this height, the countryside was so poor that the poverty was neither picturesque nor pastoral: tin-roofed shacks with dirt floors, a man pulling up the leg of his shorts to urinate on a wall, laborers wearing slippers as they pushed wheelbarrows full of bricks. When Carver rolled down his window, he discovered that the smell of the countryside was just as unpleasant, the air thick with blasts of soot from passing trucks, the rot of buffalo dung, the fermentation of the local cuisine that he found briny and nauseating. All of the sights, sounds, and smells depressed Carver, along with Claire's and Michiko's silent treatment of him, unrelenting since yesterday.

Only Legaspi was attentive, playing *Giant Steps* on the stereo, undoubtedly informed by Claire of her father's love for bebop, the way the music flowed directly from his ear canal into his bloodstream. Of all the lands Carver had encountered, he liked France and Japan the most because of the natives' enthusiastic appreciation of jazz, an admiration they extended to him. He regarded it as fate that he had met Michiko at a jazz bar in Roppongi, she a teenage waitress and he a decade older, on R & R from Okinawa, wowed by the sight of Japanese musicians sporting porkpie hats and soul patches.

"How did you sleep, Mr. Carver?"

"Not so well." Carver was pleased someone cared enough to inquire. "I kept waking up."

"Bad dreams?"

Carver hesitated. "Just restless. Confusing."

No one asked him what he had dreamed, so he said no more. They reached the demining site ten minutes later, half a kilometer off the main blacktopped road, down an earthen track to a small house and a trio of shacks on the edge of a barren acre fenced with barbed wire. As the Land Cruiser pulled up, two teenage boys leaped from hammocks strung between two jackfruit trees. Carver immediately forgot their names after the introductions. They wore oversize shorts and anomalous T-shirts, one emblazoned with the Edmonton Oilers logo, the other commemorating a 1987 Bryan Adams concert tour. The taller one's prosthetic arm was joined with the human part at the elbow, while the other's prosthetic leg extended to mid-thigh. Carver nicknamed the tall one Tom and the shorter one Jerry, the same names he and his U-Tapao roommate, a Swede from Minnesota, had bestowed on their houseboys.

"They lost them playing with cluster bomblets when they were kids," Legaspi explained. Tom and Jerry smiled shyly, their prostheses appearing to be borrowed from mannequins, the café au lait color of the plastic not an exact match for their milk chocolate skin. What spooked Carver about the detachable limbs was not just their mismatched color, but their hairlessness. "They guard the site and look after the mongooses."

"Not mongeese?" Michiko said.

"Definitely mongooses, Mrs. Carver."

The mongoose Tom fetched from one of the shacks was named Ricky, feline in size but with a more luxuriant coat of fur and the angular, wedge-shaped head of a mouse. "We use a mongoose because it is too light to trip a mine," Legaspi said. "Meanwhile, its sense of smell is acute enough to detect explosives."

Jerry carried out a pair of robots from another shack. Instead of being the sleek, stainless steel machines Carver expected, the robots were cobbled together from what looked like two tin milk shakes, joined mouth-to-mouth, each milk shake sporting a pair of legs made from rubber hose. Like a draft of horses, the two robots were harnessed side-by-side, braced front and back by iron rods. The forward rod was attached to a round blue disc the size of a Frisbee, with Ricky yoked to the blue disc via a rubber vest, the entire robot-and-mongoose affair no more than a meter long and half that in width.

"I steer the robots with this remote control." Legaspi held up a palm-sized black box of the type William had used to fly his model planes. "Ricky sniffs for the mines. The blue disc is the impediment sensor, and when it tells the robots something is blocking the way, the robots steer Ricky away from the obstacle. And when Ricky smells a mine, which he can do from three meters, he sits up."

"That's ingenious," Michiko exclaimed.

"My adviser developed it to demine in Sri Lanka. But we're experimenting with the robot and mongoose here, too."

"So what are you still testing?" said Carver.

"The legs. It's very difficult to mimic the locomotion of human or animal legs, especially over rough terrain. Having a robot vacuum your living room floor or climb some steps is completely different from having it deal with sand, or grass, or rocks, or any unexpected thing even a five-year-old knows how to get around."

The field was planted with defused landmines. At the perimeter of the field Legaspi piloted the robot and mongoose team from under a tent, under which Claire, Michiko, and Carver also stood. Tom and Jerry followed the mongoose as it scuttled over the terrain, Tom with a metal detector strapped to his back, Jerry with a quiver full of red flags. Whenever Ricky stopped and stood up on his hind legs, Tom stepped in with the metal detector to confirm the landmine's existence, and Jerry marked it with a red flag.

"A human team would take months to clear out this area," said Legaspi. The back of his linen shirt was stained with sweat, the air humid even though the sky was gray and overcast. "You could bulldoze, but that tears up the topsoil and ruins it for farming. We can clear this in a couple of weeks for a small fraction of the cost."

Carver watched Legaspi and Claire as the humanitarian jargon of cost efficiency, improvement of the land, moral obligation, employment of local technicians, and so on spooled forth. The light and focus in Claire's eyes as she watched Legaspi were the same in Michiko's when Carver told her on their first date about driving from State College to New York City to catch Thelonious Monk at the Five Spot Café on St. Mark's Place, where he stood close enough to see the yellow half-moons of Monk's cuticles against white ivory. The great man's genius had rubbed off on him enough to shine and catch hold of Michiko's gaze. It was the same with Legaspi, borrowing someone else's ideas, and this was enough for Claire.

"Do you even know who you're dealing with? You ever thought about what the DOD could do with these robots?" Carver said. The look in Legaspi's eyes was hesitant, afraid, weak, that of someone not ready to face bare-knuckled reality, the clenched iron fist of power. Legaspi's naïveté annoyed Carver profoundly. "Some brilliant guy at a university working on a defense contract will figure out a way to put a landmine on this robot. Then the Pentagon will send it into a tunnel where a terrorist is hiding."

"That's the kind of work you would do, Dad. Don't think everyone's like you."

"It's okay," Legaspi said. "I've heard this before."

"It's not okay," Claire said. "He's old and angry and bitter and he's taking it out on everyone he meets."

"I'm not angry and bitter. What am I angry about? What am I bitter about? That I'm being lectured to by a kid who thinks he's going to save the world with a tin can robot? That I have a daughter who thinks she's Vietnamese?"

"I said I have a Vietnamese soul. It's a figure of speech. It's an expression. It means I think I've found someplace where I can do some good and make up for some of the things you've done."

"I've done? What have I done?"

"You bombed this place. Have you ever thought about how many people you killed? The thousands? The tens of thousands?"

"I don't have to listen to this."

"It's not like you've ever listened to anyone before."

"You don't understand anything. We coddled you so you wouldn't have to worry about the things we worried about. Isn't that right?"

Carver turned to Michiko for support, but she was studying the ragged copse of palm trees at the far end of the model minefield. Legaspi had returned to steering Ricky, while Claire had her arms folded across her chest, daring him to walk away, exactly as he dared her when she was six, clamoring for a blond Barbie doll in a toy store. *You can sit here and cry your eyes out, young lady.* She had promptly sat down in the aisle and howled with all the grief and fury only a child or someone on the brink of death could muster. He walked out of the store then, leaving her there, and he had no choice but to walk away now.

The monsoon struck fifteen minutes later, when Carver was a few hundred meters away from the demining site, the best he could manage on the rutted road and with his bad hip. Outrage and self-pity propelled his every step. He had never explained to Claire the difficulty of precision bombing, aiming from forty thousand feet at targets the size of football fields, like dropping golf balls into a coffee cup from the roof of a house. The tonnage fell far behind his B-52 after its release, and so he had never seen his own payload explode or even drop, although he watched other planes of his squadron scattering their black seed into the wind, leaving him to imagine what he would later see on film, the bombs exploding, footfalls of an invisible giant stomping the earth.

Claire's mind wasn't complex enough to grasp the need to strike the enemy from on high in order to save fellow Americans below, much less understand his belief that God was his copilot. She was his complete opposite, joining Amnesty International in high school and marching against Desert Storm at Vassar, as if protesting made any difference at all. If it did, the help it offered was to the enemy. Although she empathized with vast masses of people she had never met, total strangers who regarded her as a stranger and who would kill her without hesitation given the chance, she did not extend any such feeling to him.

The unfairness of this absorbed Carver so much he did not notice the rapid marshaling of storm clouds until the sky grumbled. For a few seconds scattered drops of rain pinged off his forehead. Then came the deluge. Rain glued his clothing to his body, water sluicing down the back of his collar and soaking into his hiking boots. He stopped walking, unsure of whether to keep heading for the blacktop road or turn back to the demining site. The ribbon of earthen road was now the texture of peanut butter, and he sank millimeter by millimeter into its stickiness as the monsoon's onslaught continued. This was why he hadn't wanted to visit this country, a land of bad omens and misfortune so severe he wanted nothing more to do with it than fly over it. But Claire had brought him back to this red earth, and he wasn't about to run to her for help, even if he could. He slogged toward the blacktop, not a human being or an animal in sight, the dull green fields flanking him on either side. It was the middle of the afternoon, but twilight had descended with the storm clouds.

In the distance, behind him, a car honked. He lowered his head and kept walking, the downpour so intense he feared drowning if he looked up to the sky. He heard the car's old engine as it got closer, choking like a cat coughing up a hairball. With light from the high beams scattered on the raindrops falling before him, he decided that instead of ignoring them, he should raise his head in defiance. He stopped and turned, but somehow he misjudged this simple step, his right foot trapped by mud clutching at his ankle. With the high beams in his eyes, blinding him, he made another misstep, this time with his left foot, the toe coming down straight into the mud, the leg locking at the knee and his body pitching forward into the path of the car. The mud was wet and cold against his belly and face, its odor and taste evoking the soil in the distant yard of his childhood, the one where he had so often lain prone on the earth and played soldier.

It was Legaspi who helped him to his feet and into the idling Land Cruiser, Claire hovering over them with an umbrella. They put him in the backseat, shivering, Michiko using the silk scarf she had bought yesterday to wipe the mud from his eyes and face.

"We all thought you just went to sit in the car, Jimmy," she said. Legaspi started driving toward the blacktop. "What got into you?"

"I'm sixty-eight, damn it." Carver sneezed. "I'm old but I'm not dead."

"You're sixty-nine."

He was going to argue as she scrubbed at the mud around his ears, but then he realized Michiko was right. Even his own years were elusive, time ruthlessly thinning out the once-dense herd of his memories. In the rearview mirror, he saw Legaspi looking at him, and when Legaspi spoke, his voice was not unkind.

"Where did you think you were going, Mr. Carver?" When Legaspi turned on the stereo, the title track from *Giant Steps* was playing. "You don't even know where you are."

By that evening, fever had seized Carver. The dream he hadn't recounted to Legaspi came back to him in his hospital room, where he floated on his back in a black stream, his face emerging every now and again to catch glimpses of his fellow patients in the three other beds, silver-haired, aging men, tended by crowds of relatives who chattered loudly and carried bowls and other things wrapped in towels. He smelled rice porridge, a medicine whose scent was bitter, the wet dog odor of very old people. When he was submerged in the black water, images flitted by like strange illuminated fish from the canyons of the ocean. The only ones he could clearly recall later were manifested in the dream, where he had woken to find himself a passenger in a darkened airliner. Everyone else was asleep and the portholes were closed. For some reason he knew that no one was piloting the plane, and he rose and made his way forward, his skills needed. All the dozens of passengers were Asian, their eyes closed, among them the street kids and Claire's students and Tom and Jerry. Strapped to the flight attendant's jump seat by the cockpit was their tour guide from Angkor Wat, the one who had pointed to a bridge flanked by the headless statues of deities and said, in a vaguely accusatory tone, "Foreigners took the heads." Fear clutched at Carver, but when he opened the cockpit door, all he saw were the cockpit windows peering out onto the starless river of night, the empty pilot's seat waiting for him.

"Dad."

Claire was kneeling by his bedside in the dark room.

"Dad, did you say something?"

"Thirsty."

She unsealed a bottle of water and poured him a cup, holding it to his lips with one hand while propping his head with the other. He drank too eagerly and water dribbled over his lip and onto his gown. Claire lowered his head to the pillow and then wiped his chin with a napkin.

"Michiko?"

"She's at the hotel," Claire said softly. "She's been here every day, but she can't stay here at night. The floor's too hard for her to sleep on."

"How long?"

"Three days. You've had a bad fever. You have pneumonia. You have to rest, okay?" Claire sighed. "You are so stubborn. Why did you go walking by yourself?"

He shifted his weight on the mattress, where a lump of foam had worked its way under the small of his back. "I'm a fool?"

"That's true."

"Claire."

"Yes?"

"I need to use the bathroom."

He put his arms around her neck and held on tight as she leveraged him up from the bed. She smelled of strong soap and a citrus shampoo, with no hint of perfume to mask the tang of sweat. Once he was sitting on the bed with his feet on the ground, he hung an arm around her neck and let her pull him to his feet. Claire was the right size for him to lean on, her head rising a bit over his shoulder, his arm draping comfortably over her back. She kicked aside a bamboo mat on the floor and maneuvered him down the narrow passage between his bed and his neighbor's. "Careful, Dad," Claire said, steering him past a body stretched out on the floor and curled up under a sheet, head turned away from him. "You'll be okay. You just need some rest."

What she wanted to say, but wouldn't, was that he should not be frightened. He was not going to die here. But he was frightened, more so than he had ever expected to be. Before Michiko and the children, he believed he would die in an airplane or behind the wheel of a very fast car, anything involving high velocity and a sudden, arresting stop. Now he knew he would probably die with panic pooling in his lungs, in a place where he was not supposed to be, on the wrong side of the world. He hung on to Claire even more tightly as she clutched him around his waist, navigating him past the first body and around another at the foot of a bed by the door. When he tripped on the body's outstretched foot, a woman with short-cropped hair raised her head and snapped, "Troi oi, can than di!" To which Claire said, apologetically, "Xin loi, co!"

The woman must be a relative of one of the patients, or maybe a patient herself. Claire must have been sleeping on the bamboo mat by his bed. The realization burned through the fog of dizziness and fear, delivering a feeling for his daughter so strong it pained him. He remembered her infancy, when Michiko insisted on sleeping with Claire in between them, he so worried about rolling over in his sleep onto Claire that he lay awake restless until he could worry no more, whereupon he climbed down to the floor and slept on the carpet. Not so many years later, when Claire was walking but barely potty-trained, and still sleeping in their bed, she would wake up, slip off the edge and land on his chest, and when he opened one eye, demand to be taken to the bathroom. The trip alone in the dark was too frightening. He would sigh, get up, and lead her down the hall, step by careful step, her hand wrapped around one of his fingers.

"Dad," Claire said. The bathroom door was a pale green rectangle in the blue moonlight before them. "Dad, are you crying?"

"No, baby, I'm not," he said, even though he was.

SOMEONE ELSE BESIDES YOU

My father's girlfriend lived in a condo complex made to look like a village, the stucco barracks scattered around a flat lawn spotted with barbecue pits. Behind one of the barracks a leaf blower whined as I followed my father along a winding brick path, past a swimming pool that smelled of chlorine, and up an echoing stairway. We stopped on the second floor, and my father used a key linked on the chain of his Swiss Army knife to unlock a condo door. When he called out her name—Mimi—it was the first time I'd heard it.

Mimi was sitting on a white leather couch in the living room, using a remote control to dial down the volume on the television backed into one corner. She stood up, and if she was surprised to see me, she didn't show it. Her plum velour tracksuit fitted snugly on her slender body. Photographs of my mother before she was married show that she was once slim too, but by the end of her life everything about her had thickened and sagged, except for her fading hair. When she died, she was wearing the wig I'd given to her for a birthday present, woven from real human hair. Mimi's perm resembled the wig, except that Mimi's hair was naturally rich and abundant, rooted to her head in auburn waves, the style of a woman in her fifties.

"I've been waiting to meet you for so long!" she said, clasping both my hands in hers. The skin of her face was beige and unnaturally smooth, like nylon stockings.

"Thanks," I said. Singing on the television was a girl with crimped hair, wearing a black vinyl bodice and a red leather miniskirt. Above the television was a faded lacquer version of the Last Supper, with Jesus and the disciples framed in pink neon. My father bumped into me on his way to the couch, and I said, "I've heard a lot about you."

My father turned the volume up on the television. "He wants to pee."

"Of course." Mimi kept smiling as she led me down the hall to the bathroom, where I grimaced at her before I closed the door. The bathroom was immaculate and scented with potpourri, unlike the ones in the rented houses where I'd grown up, which always smelled vaguely of mildewed plastic shower curtains and ammonia. After a decent interval, I flushed the toilet. In the car I had told my father that I needed to use the bathroom only so I could see this woman's face, and how she lived. When I checked her medicine cabinet, all I found were aspirin, beauty creams, and several varieties of nail polish. I'd expected a sample packet of Viagra, like the one my ex-wife Sam once found in my father's toiletry kit after he asked her, without thinking, to fetch him his nail clippers.

When I returned to the living room, the television was off, and my father was reading the paper as he sat on the couch. Mimi was preparing coffee at the bar dividing the living room from the kitchen, where a skylight illuminated her stainless-steel oven and electric range. My mother had cooked on a vintage gas oven and stove with a pilot light that kept going out, and when an aneurysm struck her down last year at the age of fifty-three, she was working in the kitchen. I think it was the surprise of her dying so young that bowed my father down at the funeral, rather than grief or the shock of having found her lying on the linoleum floor, a pot of chicken bones simmering on the burner.

"Do you want milk with your coffee?" Mimi asked.

"I'm sorry," I said. "I have to go."

"But you just came. And I have biscotti and croissants."

"I only came to drop my father off." Above the fireplace was a black-and-white photograph framed in rosewood, of a gaunt man in his sixties, wearing spectacles and a dark suit. "His car was stolen last night."

"So I heard. That's what comes from living in Los Angeles." Mimi noticed me looking at the photograph. "My husband passed away five years ago. He was a senator once, you know."

"He has to go." My father put the newspaper down and stood up. "The boy has two jobs."

I was thirty-three, but my father didn't think anyone was a man until he fathered children. He'd had five with my mother. All three sons had grown taller than him, but most people, including me, tended to forget his height. People noticed only that he was a broad-chested man with muscular forearms that were still as thick as they were when I hung from them as a kid. His body remained trim enough to fit into the vintage camouflage paratrooper's uniform that he'd worn during the war. These days he broke out the uniform only once every few months, to march in the honor guard for parades and memorials in Little Saigon. He always did so with the intense stare that Sam remembered from their first meeting, when she found she couldn't look away from him, as if she were a wild animal transfixed by the gaze of a wilder one.

Perhaps Mimi felt the same way. Her eyes were on my father as she said to me, "Come by for dinner anytime." For a moment I believed she meant it.

My father walked me to the door and pointed a finger at his compass watch. Its face was the size of a silver dollar, the body and band scratched but still as tough as the day he'd gotten it in 1958, at the Fort Benning airborne school. "I'll need a ride back tomorrow morning," he said. Then he closed the door in my face.

"Sure," I said. "You're welcome."

I was used to the way he was spare with most things in his life, from his words to his '82 Honda hatchback. When he'd come to my apartment six weeks ago, everything he owned was in the car, which was original down to the push-button radio that picked up only static-thick AM channels. Wanting to be helpful, I'd reached for a suitcase. The moment I tried to lift it, I knew I'd made a mistake. It must have contained his dumbbells, and the seconds ticked by silently as I struggled with both hands to drag the suitcase out of the trunk. When I'd finally gotten the suitcase to the sidewalk, he sighed and took it from me, lifting it with one arm and bracing it against his hip. Then he slung his duffel bag over the other shoulder and turned to the stairs. He swung the suitcase up each step with the aid of his leg, leaving me with the garment bags. Last month he'd turned sixty-three, and every grunt he gave punctuated what I should have known already. Living with him now would be harder than it was during my childhood.

All through the morning, while I processed refunds and listened in on my service representatives, I pictured my father and Mimi lounging on the white leather couch, watching the Vietnamese channel on television. Mimi was the first of my father's mistresses and girlfriends that I'd seen, the mysterious women that my mother screamed about to my father behind their bedroom door when my brothers and sisters and I were younger. Now I had a face and a name for the woman sitting next to my father under the gaze of her husband. My father hadn't even put up my mother's picture, as custom said he should have, next to the photographs of his dead parents on his dresser.

I found it soothing during my lunch break to call Sam's home number and listen to her answering machine. "Hey there, stranger," she said. "You know what to do." Teaching geometry to tenth-graders had trained her to speak in a gentle and pleasant way. Sam was popular with her students, like my father with his. He was a high school guidance counselor, and every Christmas, alumni would send dozens of cards to the man they affectionately called Mr. P, updating him on their careers and families. I doubted if Mr. P's students ever imagined that he had mistresses, or that once, in his past, he'd jumped out of airplanes and commanded a battalion of paratroopers. To the students, he'd merely say that he'd been a soldier once. He was a modest man who didn't like to talk about his other life with acquaintances or his own children any more than I told my coworkers about how, at the end of the day, I drove to a convenience store parking lot and changed in the front seat, wriggling into gray slacks and a red polyester blazer. My coworkers knew me to be a customer service manager for a company in Burbank that sold hearing aids, oxygen tanks, and motorized wheelchairs, but by night I was a watchman at a luxury high-rise on the Wilshire Corridor near UCLA. No one could say I was lazy, as Sam had conceded during one of our arguments last year.

The job was perfect, because after Sam left me and my mother died, I could no longer sleep. Nights at the high-rise were quiet and didn't require much of me. Every now and then I got up to walk the hallways, stairways, and underground parking garage, but mostly I sat in the marble lobby, watching every corner of the building on a bank of video monitors. When I wasn't reading one of the several newspapers I'd brought, I played solitaire. In between games I would draw a random card from the deck, and if it was the ace of spades, I called Sam. If she answered the phone, I said nothing, waiting to see how many times she said "Hello?" before she hung up.

She was a patient woman, but her patience ran out last year, when she turned thirty-four. We had gone to Palms Thai restaurant on Hollywood for her birthday, because she was a fan of the Thai Elvis who shimmied and shimmered onstage in a different costume each night. That evening, he was wearing a gold lamé pantsuit as he sang a passable version of "(Let Me Be Your) Teddy Bear," pushing rose-tinted sunglasses up his nose with a jeweled finger every now and then.

"I want a child, Thomas." Sam tucked a long strand of hair behind her ear, almost shyly. "And I want to have it with you." The strand was dyed purple, while the rest of her hair was its natural brunette. A diamond stud the size of a pinhead glittered above her left nostril, and my initials were tattooed in blue ink on her right wrist, serving as a reminder of me, she said, whenever she checked the time. For some reason her rebelliousness had charmed my father, so much so that after our divorce, he said I was to blame.

"I don't know if I'm ready yet," I told Sam. This wasn't the first time we'd had this conversation. "I don't know if I'll be good with children."

"Get over it, Thomas. You're not going to turn out like your father."

My father was someone who, for the better part of a decade, woke my brothers and me from our sofa bed at dawn to perform calisthenics with him. We did push-ups with one of our sisters sitting on our backs, and sit-ups clutching a Webster's unabridged dictionary to our chests. We ran through an obstacle course of old tires in the backyard and used the branch of an oak tree for chin-ups, straining and grunting until we fell off the limb. After that, we practiced marksmanship with a BB gun, plinking away at Budweiser cans filled with sand. Then we ran for miles, not stopping until one of us vomited, proof that my father was succeeding in his goal of making us into men.

"He's insane." I thought Sam would see the risks. "Aren't you worried I'll start my own army? Or keep a girlfriend on the side?"

"Like I said." Sam poured herself a glass of water from the pitcher on the table. "You're not your father."

My shift ended at dawn. It was a forty-minute drive from the Westside to my Eastside apartment, on a side street off the up-and-coming stretch of Sunset, not far from where the boulevard became César Chávez. Stolen cars and hovering police helicopters were commonplace here in Echo Park, where I'd moved after the divorce. By the time my mother passed away during the summer, I knew what loneliness was like, and on the day after the funeral, suspecting my father might be lonely too, I invited him to come live with me. I hadn't expected him to say yes.

Today was my day off from both jobs, but after sleeping for only two hours, I got up, showered, shaved, and dressed in fifteen minutes. Half an hour later, I had crossed from Echo Park to Mimi's neighborhood, the Chinese mecca on Atlantic and Valley boulevards. She opened the door wearing a pink velour tracksuit. My father was showering after his morning run, and she insisted on preparing me a cup of coffee. I heard him singing in the bathroom as Mimi returned with a glass of ice in one hand and, in the other, a second glass with the condensed milk, a stainless steel filter perched on top. While we waited for the black coffee to drip, she smiled and said, "Your father speaks highly of you."

"Not as highly as he speaks of you."

"He says you work in the medical industry."

"I sell hearing aids. In the evenings I'm a night watchman at a high-rise."

"I see." We heard the running water stop.

"It's an expensive apartment building," I offered. "The women wear fur coats just because they can afford to."

When Mimi smiled at me again, a gold tooth glinted in the far reaches of her mouth. "It's not good for a boy your age to be without a woman," she said. "Your father tells me you're not even dating."

"I'm recovering."

Mimi ignored my comment and began describing the young women she knew at her temple, as well as the ones from her old neighborhood in Can Tho, everyone searching for husbands with American passports. Vietnamese women, she informed me, leaning close and putting her hand on my knee, were much better mates for men than American women, who were fickle and demanding. Vietnamese women took care of their men, doted on them, and these same women wanted men like me, neither too American nor too Vietnamese. She nodded at my father, who had appeared in the doorway, already dressed in a button-down shirt and wrinkle-free slacks. Ignoring her, he looked at me and said, "Today we're going to rent a car."

"Are you coming back tonight?" Mimi asked.

"Tomorrow," he said. "Now hurry up and drink your coffee before the ice melts."

As soon as I'd finished, he ushered me out. He said nothing to me in the car, jingling the keys in his pocket until we came to a complete stop where the Harbor and Hollywood freeways crossed. A squadron of news helicopters circled lazily over the freeway some distance toward downtown, its towers only ghostly silhouettes hidden by a curtain of smog. I lit a cigarette, and my father rolled down his window. After my mother died, he quit his pack-a-day habit, even though she'd never objected to his secondhand smoke; she just complained about the migraines that forced her to turn off the lights in her bedroom and lie down. "It's my head," she would moan. "It's my head."

"When was the last time you talked to her?" he asked.

"Who?" I thought he meant my mother.

"Sam."

"Months ago." I blew smoke out the window. "She called to say she was sorry about Ma."

"How will you get her back if you don't talk to her?"

"None of your business."

"You give up too easy." Sam told me the same thing soon after we first met, our senior year in college. "Look at you," he said.

I checked myself. "What about me?"

"You've gained weight. You haven't combed your hair." He plucked at my pants. "And you haven't ironed your clothing. A man must always iron his clothing."

"I thought Ma pressed your clothes."

"The point is that you look terrible." He slapped his hand against the dashboard for emphasis. "How many of those cigarettes are you smoking every day?"

"Six or seven."

"Put it out." When I did nothing, he snatched the cigarette out of my mouth and tossed it out the window, then grabbed a handful of the fat around my waist, squeezing it hard. "You even feel like a woman."

"Jesus Christ!" I pushed his hand away. "Don't do that!"

"You're never getting Sam back looking that way."

"Who says I want her back?"

"Don't be an idiot. You were only half a man before you met her, and you're back to being half a man now."

Through my window, I could see into the low-slung Mitsubishi next to us, where miniature television screens, embedded in customized headrests, broadcast a scene of a crowded highway. The camera zoomed in on a team of highway patrolmen in tan uniforms with their guns drawn, surrounding a car. It was our highway, captured live from a news helicopter.

"What about you?" I said. "Are you going to marry that woman? And then find yourself another one on the side?"

Someone behind me began honking, and soon cars all over the freeway took up the noise. I remembered my mother pulling me aside once, when I was eleven or twelve, demanding to know where my father disappeared to on Friday nights. I had no idea. For some reason her question terrified me more than the time she chased him into the bathroom. When he locked the door against her, she tried to beat it down with a chair, the legs leaving fist-sized holes in the hollow door.

"Sam's a good woman." My father reached over and pressed the horn once, twice, and a third time. "You should never have let her go."

As if to prove how little of a man I was, I started crying.

My father stared straight ahead, and I knew he must be thinking of the funeral. He hadn't shed a tear during the mass, and neither had I, but when I drove him from the church to the cemetery, something broke inside me, and the tears gushed out. My father had stopped speaking then, too. He was worried, I think, about the chances of my crashing the car. Only when I finished crying did he resume talking about the wake. But today, with horns honking all around, my father sighed and said, "That's enough. It's time we did something about you."

Traffic began moving. The horns stopped, and my father turned on the radio, picking a soft-rock station where Paul McCartney and Stevie Wonder were singing "Ebony and

Ivory." I didn't know what he meant by "doing something," which was what he said whenever he was about to punish my brothers or me. It was also what he said the time I came home one day in the fourth grade and reported that a kid up the street had spat on the lunch of sardines and rice my mother had packed. Then the kid called me a slant-eyed fag.

My father wasn't yet a high school guidance counselor at that time. He was a night-shift janitor in a downtown office building and a part-time student at Cal State L.A. Wearing his janitor's uniform, he made me walk him from our apartment to the other boy's house, where I waited on the sidewalk as my father went up the stoop and knocked on the front door. The man who came onto the porch was taller than my father by six or seven inches, and wore a mechanic's blue overalls unzipped to the bottom of his paunch. Curly brown hair sprouted from the back of his hands, and over the top of his T-shirt, and from his ears—everywhere except for the top of his head.

I didn't hear what they said, both of them speaking in low, angry tones, until the moment the other father said, "Like hell I will." My father kicked him in the groin without another word or warning, and, when the man doubled over, punched him in the throat. After the man fell facedown onto the porch, I saw his son standing behind the screen door, wide-eyed. My father didn't bother looking behind him as he walked back toward me. There was no joy or excitement on his face as he put his hand on my shoulder, and for a moment I thought he was going to make me fight the man's son. But all he did with that hand was to steer me home, gently patting me the entire way, saying nothing.

We picked up a rental car from the Enterprise lot in Los Feliz, a Ford the size of a golf cart and only a little more powerful. Then my father took me to his barbershop in old Chinatown, in an alley off Broadway, where a man with orange hair and a studded belt ran clippers through my hair and chuckled over his good times with the twenty-dollar whores in Saigon. After he was finished, I wasn't sure which was uglier, the rented Ford or my haircut, so short I looked as if I'd been discharged from the army. I could feel the breeze on my scalp that evening, blowing in over Baldwin Hills to Sam's doorstep. She had moved here after the divorce, to a town house on the heights above La Cienega, overlooking a field of oil derricks.

"This is a mistake," I said.

He knocked on the door. "We haven't seen her in a long time, and we're just going to talk."

My father had said we would have the advantage of surprise, even though we were on Sam's territory. But he was getting old, because this was the extent of his plan to do something about me. He'd forgotten to reconnoiter or prepare for a worst-case scenario. Still, even if he had remembered, I don't think he could have been prepared for the fact that when Sam opened the door, she would be wearing a maternity dress with ruffles of crepe-like material, making her swollen belly look like a piñata.

"Oh," she said. Her hair was shorn into a blond pageboy, its brown roots showing. "You're the last people I expected to see."

"You're pregnant," I said.

"It's kind of you to notice, Thomas. Hi, Mr. P."

"Well," my father said. "Look at you."

"It's good seeing you, too." Behind her, someone was talking on the television in the living room. "I don't mean to be rude, but you should have called."

"We were just taking a drive," I said. "And we thought we'd stop by."

Sam knew my father and I never drove together just for fun, but she beckoned us in anyway. I expected another man to be there and entered cautiously, checking either side before stepping in. Stacks of student exams were arranged by grade on the avocado shag carpet, at the chrome feet of a couch made from fake black leather that we'd shopped for together in the Korean shops on Western Avenue. "Sorry for the mess," Sam said, easing herself onto the couch.

My father occupied the armchair, and I was forced to sit on the far end of the couch from hers. I toed a stack of exams, one with a red "C" on the topmost sheet. "They're not doing so well."

"I think I'm losing my touch," she replied.

People say a pregnant woman glows in a beautiful way with love and expectation. I'd always imagined this glow as a kind of aura, but the shine on Sam's puffy face was only a reflection from a glaze of oil and sweat. "I'm not as energetic in the classroom as I usually am," she went on. "It's rubbing off on the students."

"A teacher must lead by example," my father remarked.

"So you've always said, Mr. P." She closed her eyes for a moment, as if she were tired. "If you'd like a beer, you can help yourself. Getting me up almost requires a crane."

"You have beer?" I said.

"I keep it for guests."

We should have refused out of politeness, but my father immediately went to the kitchen for the beer. Sam rested her hands on her belly and gave me a neutral look. "What have you been doing, Thomas?"

"Working. And sleeping."

"Me, too."

"My father moved in with me."

She laughed. "That must be interesting. Who does the cooking?"

"He's the cook, of course." My father returned with two bottles of beer, a bowl of pretzels, and a glass of water. "The master of instant noodles."

"Thanks, Mr. P," Sam said when my father handed her the glass. "I need to cool down. I'm having a hot flash."

We lapsed into silence and watched the show on television, about the cruelty of the meat industry's practices. When my father broke the silence and complimented her on the house, Sam explained that most of the decorations belonged to her roommate, another teacher who was out for the night. My father pointed the tip of his beer bottle at the television, on top of which was a pipe, carved from teak and in the shape of a dragon with a ball of opium in its mouth. "From where did you buy that?"

"Hue." She spoke the city's name with the correct rising accent. "But you can't actually smoke anything with it."

"You went to Vietnam?" my father and I said at the same time.

"Last summer. I didn't teach summer school and went backpacking instead. Sometimes"—she paused—"a girl just needs a vacation."

"Did you think about me?" I said.

Sam shifted her weight on the couch, uncrossing and crossing her legs, the ankles and calves swollen. "Of course I thought about you." She smiled at me as if I was one of her students. Then she looked at my father, who was studying the cottage cheese ceiling. "And you, too, Mr. P."

"I will never go back." He rapped his bottle of beer on the coffee table. "You do not know the Communists. I know the Communists."

"They're not so bad. They just want to move on with their lives."

My father shook his head emphatically. "You are a foreigner. You know nothing. They take your money and say nice things to you."

"Maybe you should go back," Sam said quietly. "You can get closure."

"I will never go back." My father slashed his index finger across his throat and made a guttural noise. "If I go back, they will call me a war criminal. They will put me in reeducation, and you will never hear from me again."

Sam pushed herself off the couch, rising before my father got started about what evil the Communists had done or would do. He would tell these stories for an entire evening. "Excuse me," Sam said. "I have to use the bathroom."

After she left, my father turned to me and hissed, motioning to his belly and making a round curve in the air with his hand. I ignored him and got up to look around the living room for traces of a man. All I saw were the trappings of our life together. I'd given Sam everything when we divorced except half the money, but I hadn't expected her to keep our mementos on display. Above the mantel were figurines of hula dancers from our honeymoon in Hawaii, and on a bookshelf were crystal paperweights in the shape of dolphins we'd bought in Puerto Vallarta. By the heater was the Robert Doisneau print I'd bought her in senior year, the black-and-white one with the man and woman kissing on a Parisian street.

Next to the paperweights was a lacquered jewelry box etched with mother-of-pearl, which I assumed she'd bought in Vietnam. We'd talked often about visiting, but I'd never really wanted to go. I wasn't even born there, my mother having given birth to me at a refugee camp in Guam, where my father named me after the American adviser who'd given him the compass watch. I didn't understand what drew Sam to Vietnam, except maybe a need to find closure of her own. Perhaps she'd found it. She seemed happy when she brought out two envelopes of photos from her trip and told us the stories behind them. "A beautiful country," she said, which was what everyone said about it. "Poor and hot, but beautiful."

Despite himself, my father grunted in pleasure as he studied the pictures. Sam had landed in Saigon and traveled north to Hue and Hanoi, with detours to Ha Long Bay and the mountains of Sapa. Most of these were places he'd only read about, since the war had kept his generation from seeing their own country. He passed me a picture of Sam on the deck of a boat, wearing a safari hat and a powder-blue North Face hiking jersey, the one I'd bought her for Christmas. Her freckles had faded to invisibility against her skin, pink from the sun, and she was leaning into a man with sandy-blond dreadlocks draped on his shoulders.

"Is this the father?" I jabbed at the man's face with my finger.

She sighed. "Please don't be stupid, Thomas."

"It's just a question."

"You had a chance, Thomas. We had a chance."

My father said, "Excuse me," got up, and walked out the front door without another word. After the door closed, Sam shook her head and said, "Neither of you has changed one bit."

"I wouldn't say that."

"How have you changed, Thomas? Besides your haircut?"

"You're the one who's changing." My voice was loud. "You're changing the subject."

"A woman can have a baby by herself." Her tone of voice didn't rise as it used to when we fought, but stayed subdued, as if weighed down by the unborn child. "A woman doesn't need a man to be the father of her child, Thomas."

"You might as well say the earth is flat."

"Oh, my God." She stretched the words out sarcastically, imitating the way the students spoke in her classes, the ones she used to talk about over dinner. "What century are you living in?"

I wanted to ask her what a woman is without a husband, what a child is without a father, what a boy is without a man, but the questions wouldn't come out. "Who's the father?" I said.

"You don't have any right to ask me that."

Perhaps it was another teacher, or somebody she met on the Internet, or a stranger she got drunk with in a bar one night. Perhaps it was even some lucky Vietnamese tour guide. The thought of these other men made me drink the rest of the beer, not so much for the taste as to give me something to do besides throw the bottle into the television. When I was done, Sam got up and walked to the door, leaving me no choice but to follow. My foot was on the threshold when the unexpected sound of my name caused me to turn around, hopeful.

"Don't come back, Thomas," she said. Over her shoulder, the television narrator was intoning about corporate pipelines and Nigerian strongmen. "You know it's not good for either one of us."

My father was waiting for me in the Ford, smoking a cigarette from the pack of Camels I'd left on the dash. The stereo was on, and because American music didn't please him, he'd brought along a CD of melancholic ballads sung by Khanh Ly. He liked to say that whenever he listened to her, it might as well be 1969 all over again. I got into the car and turned off the stereo. The street was empty and quiet, except for the hum of traffic from La Cienega and the barking of a dog somewhere up the hill.

"That was a great idea," I said.

He tossed the cigarette out the window. "So did she tell you who the man is?"

"She wouldn't say." I released the brake and eased the Ford into the street, lined with cars parked bumper to bumper. Halfway down the street, he said, "Stop." Sam's Toyota was next to us, pointing downhill with its wheels turned to the curb. The car was weathered and gray, and on the dusty rear window someone had drawn a frowning face.

"Kill the lights," my father said. He waited until I turned them off before he slipped out his Swiss Army knife and got out of the car. After walking once around the Toyota, he knelt down and braced himself against the driver's side wheel well with his left arm, the knife in his right hand. He drove the knife hard into the tire, working the short blade against the rubber for several seconds until the incision was several inches wide. If the knife made a sound when it came out of the tire, I didn't hear it.

Once he'd repeated his work on the other three tires, he snapped the knife shut, stood up, and inspected the car with his hands on his hips. I looked over my shoulder, up and down the street, but the sidewalk was empty, and though some windows were lit with the blue glow of televisions, no one was looking out. When I turned back to the Toyota, my father was gone, and for a moment I'd thought he'd run away. But then he rose into my vision from the other side of the Toyota, a rock the size of a grapefruit in his hand. He hefted the rock over his head, paused to check his balance, and then hurled it at the car, throwing his whole body behind it. The windshield of the car cracked and buckled under the impact, but the sagging glass held, cradling the rock even as the echo bounced up and down the hill.

When he climbed back into the car, I said, "You're crazy, you know that?"

"Just drive." He spoke through gritted teeth. "Don't turn on the lights until you get to the bottom of the hill."

I waited until I turned the corner before I flipped on the headlights and accelerated. "I don't know you." I banged the wheel with my fist. "I don't know why anyone would do something like that."

"She'll blame it on the blacks."

All the cars around us had black drivers.

"That's not what I meant."

"So why didn't you say something?" My father leaned his head against the headrest and closed his eyes. "You should have rolled down the window and stopped me. You could have honked your horn, made people come to their windows."

We drove past the oil derricks, visible as shadows in the shape of gigantic pelicans nesting. Until Sam moved to Baldwin Hills, I hadn't known Los Angeles even had oil. But

I guess oil was to be found in every part of the world, just like anger and sorrow. A person only had to know where to look. I said, "No one has ever told you anything that would stop you, not from doing something you wanted."

"That's because everything I've ever done I believed in." The car hit a bump on the entrance ramp to the Santa Monica Freeway, and he cursed, clasping his hand to his neck as if a bullet had grazed him.

"What's wrong?"

He opened his eyes. "I think I pulled a muscle."

"Serves you right."

"You wouldn't know right from wrong." There was no trace of anger in his voice. "The only way a man knows right from wrong is when he makes a choice."

"So was it right to cheat on Ma?" Far ahead of us, the sparse lights of downtown's towers glittered. "Was it right to drive her to her grave the way you did? Do you believe you did the right thing?"

My father sighed the way he did all those mornings of my childhood when he came into the living room and saw us asleep, or pretending to be asleep, hoping he might forget to drag us out of bed. I waited for him to clip me on the ear or sucker punch me for what I said, but he didn't. He kept quiet until we were driving through downtown, when he said, "I never loved your mother."

"I don't want to hear it."

"But I respected her," he continued. "She was dutiful. She was a good woman. My father chose her for me because

she was a virtuous girl, even though he knew I loved someone else. And this is why I never chose any woman for you.
I wanted you to find a woman you loved."

"Don't make this about me."

"Who else is it about?"

He closed his eyes once more, and from downtown to
the apartment, we didn't speak again. When we reached his
bedroom, I had to help him take off his shirt and lie down,
holding him by the shoulders while he braced his neck and
head. I saw the six-inch scar on his chest that I'd sometimes
seen as a child, after he'd come out of the shower with a towel
around his waist. Since he never told us anything about what
he'd done in the war, we made up stories about how he'd been
shot through the chest, or stabbed by the husband of one of
his mistresses. The scar was a vivid bolt of red lightning in
my memory, angled between his sternum and his heart, but
in the dim light of his bedroom, it was only a pink zipper
holding the rumpled, loose skin of his chest together.

I found sleeping pills in a drawer of his nightstand, along
with a bottle of eucalyptus oil and a box of Salonpas. "Take
one," I said, dropping a pill into his mouth. He swallowed it
without water and I rolled him over, because even that act required a man to use the muscles of his neck. I splashed some
of the eucalyptus oil onto his shoulders and neck and began
massaging him. Soon enough he was breathing evenly, and
once he was asleep, I bandaged him with the white strips of
Salonpas, their medicinal scent reminding me of the times

when he would lay them upon me after particularly hard mornings of exercise.

After I was done, I picked up his shirt and opened the closet. The hanger was in my hand when I glanced at the shelf above the closet rod and saw my mother's wig, resting on its Styrofoam head. What compelled him to save this, of all things, was beyond me. I hung up the shirt quickly and turned off the lights before I went to my room. There I lay in bed, listening for the police helicopters that cruised overhead almost every night or the Spanish rock that was always floating up from the crowded evangelical church down the hill. But everything was so strangely still and quiet, I thought I wasn't even in my own apartment, and when I closed my eyes I saw the head's oval face once again, marked by an arched nose and thin lips, its expression white, blank, and eyeless as it gazed down upon me.

Late the following day, the police found my father's Honda on a side street of Boyle Heights. The next morning, while I was sleeping between shifts, my father went with Mimi to retrieve it from the impound lot. They returned by the time I was awake and drinking my coffee, black and without sugar. My father was whistling a tune I didn't recognize when he opened the door, Mimi trailing behind him. "Miracles do happen after all," he said. "The car's in one piece. The police think it was just stolen by kids looking for a joyride."

"Lucky you," I said.

"The little bastards even left me a gift." He chuckled and showed me a cheap removable stereo in his palm, his movement stiff and awkward from his strained neck. "I guess they couldn't stand the radio."

"The stereo's probably stolen, too."

"If the police don't have a problem with it, then neither do I."

After he went outside with a vacuum cleaner and rags to clean up the car, I was left alone with Mimi. She sat on the edge of the futon, wearing a purple satin tracksuit with clean white sneakers, hands folded on her lap as she smiled at me. The early morning sun coming through the living room windows reflected off the satin and illuminated her in the halo of dust floating up from the futon. Seeing her with my father made me think that perhaps Sam had made the right choice after all. Perhaps she was thinking of my father and mother when she divorced me. Perhaps she knew then what I know now, that they never should have married each other. The truth of the matter was that my father and mother should have married other people, even though, in that case, I might never have been born.

"Sometimes I feel so sorry for you bachelors," she said.

"Mimi."

"My housekeeper does a great job," she went on. "She's looking for some more work in case you need help cleaning."

"Aunt Mimi," I said. The coffee's bitterness only made me aware of how dull my mind was.

"She cooks, too, nearly as good as I can."

"You know he's going to cheat on you, don't you?"

For a moment she said and did nothing, her expression unchanging. I thought she might not have heard me, or if she had, that she was too shocked even to react. Then she stood up, brushing away the cloud of dust with a wave of her hand. I expected her to say something, perhaps how she was not like my mother, but she didn't say a word. Instead, she walked to the door without looking at me, her smile fixed on her face, and for a moment I believed she might just ignore me. But, with her hand on the doorknob, she stopped and turned to look at me.

"Tell me something," she said. The curve of her smile straightened into a thin, hard line. "Aren't there times when you'd rather be someone else besides you?"

I went to work. Then I changed my clothes and went to work again. Near dawn of the next day, I came home from night duty and was so tired that I wasn't even aware of crossing the threshold of my bedroom and falling asleep, not until a staccato pounding woke me up after what seemed like only minutes. Someone was knocking on the front door. The alarm clock said it was seven thirty, and when I looked down, I saw that I was still wearing my pants. My shirt and shoes were on the carpet. I waited for my father to answer the door, but when the pounding only became more insistent, I had to climb out of bed.

Whoever it was kept beating on the front door until I opened it. Sam was standing there, right hand raised and clenched. She was wearing an unbuttoned red cardigan over a black top and matching black pants made of stretchable wool. Her pregnant belly protruded over her waistband, and her top had ridden up, leaving an eye-shaped sliver of her flesh exposed. The navel at its center was like a pupil, its iris the gold belly ring she'd acquired in her freshman year one drunken night.

"I didn't know you had it in you," she said, brushing by me.

The sunlight behind her was blinding. I blinked and said, "What?"

"My car!" She pivoted in the middle of the living room to face me. "I spent all day yesterday getting it fixed. How could you do that? How?"

My watchman's jacket was thrown onto the armchair by the door, and in the breast pocket was an envelope full of cash that I had gotten from the bank during lunch yesterday. My plan had been to slide the unmarked envelope under her door that evening. I took the envelope out of the jacket and offered it to her.

"What's that?" she said, arms folded above her belly.

"It's enough to pay for the car."

Sam looked at the envelope for a moment and hesitated. I kept myself very still. If I so much as shook the envelope or said another word, she'd refuse it and curse me on her way out. While she was making up her mind, the sight of her belly ring and the smooth, tight canopy of flesh it rooted on transfixed me. I wondered if she'd named the baby yet, if she knew its sex, and, above all, if she'd told the man who was going to be the father.

"When I saw what you'd done to the car, part of me wanted to kill you," Sam said, taking the envelope. "But another part of me thought you cared in some strange, screwed-up way that was completely your own."

I stepped forward and put my hand on her belly.

"Mostly I wanted to kill you," she said, frowning.

I leaned closer and put my other hand on her belly, the navel and the ring between my two hands. I waited for the baby to kick or to turn over in the womb, and when nothing happened, I knelt down and placed my ear against Sam's belly. There was a life hidden there, a life that if I were to hold it in my hands would weigh almost nothing. When I spoke, it was so softly that only the stranger curled up behind the belly ring could hear. Then I said it once more, louder: "I can be the father." Feeling Sam's hand grip my shoulder, I said it a third time, just to make sure they both heard me right.

"Stand up, Thomas," she said. "I want you to stand up."

I stood up. We faced each other, her belly buffering us.

"Do you know what you're saying?" she asked. "Do you have any idea what you're doing?"

"I have absolutely no idea," I said. Sam bit her lip and looked down, but she didn't back away. I saw a pattern of three age spots by her jawbone. They had not been there the year before, when we had drawn up the divorce agreement with pen and paper, without lawyers and with a bottle of wine. I traced the slope of her cheek to the jaw, where the age spots were arranged like the dots on a die. A floorboard creaking in my father's room announced that he had crept out of bed and was undoubtedly standing against the door. Sam and I turned our heads to the sound, but we heard nothing more. He was waiting, just like us, for what was to come.

FATHERLAND

*I*t was a most peculiar thing to do, or so everyone said on hearing the story of how Phuong's father had named his second set of children after his first. Phuong was the eldest of these younger children, and for all of her twenty-three years she had believed that her father's other children were much more blessed. Evidence of their good fortune was written in the terse letters sent home annually by the mother of Phuong's namesake, the first Mrs. Ly, who enumerated each of her children's accomplishments, height, and weight in bullet points. Phuong's namesake, for example, was seven years older, fifteen centimeters taller, twenty kilos heavier, and, from the record in the photographs included with the letters, in possession of fairer, clearer skin; a thinner, straighter nose; and hair, clothing, shoes, and makeup that only became ever more fashionable as she graduated from a private girls' school, then from an elite college, followed by medical school and then a residency in Chicago. Mr. Ly had laminated each of the photographs to protect them from humidity and fingerprints, keeping them neatly stacked on a side table by the couch in the living room.

The letters accompanying the photographs were the only communiqués that Phuong's family received about the children, for over the course of some twenty-seven years' absence, Phuong's namesake and her two younger brothers had never written a word themselves. And so, when the first such letter finally arrived, it was the cause of a great deal of excitement. The letter was addressed to Mr. Ly, who, as the plenipotentiary of the house, always took it upon himself to open the mail. He sat on the couch and slit the envelope carefully, using one of the few relics from his past he had managed to keep, a silver letter opener with an ivory handle. Flanking him were Phuong and her mother, while his two teenage sons, Hanh and Phuc, sat on the armrests and craned their necks to catch a glimpse of the words their father read out loud. The letter was even shorter than the ones written by the ex-wife, merely announcing that Phuong's half sister would be coming for a two-week vacation, and that she hoped to stay with them.

"Vivien?" Mrs. Ly said, reading the name signed at the bottom of the letter. "Is she too good to use the name you gave her?"

But Phuong knew instantly why her sister had taken upon herself a foreign name, and whose name it must have been: Vivien Leigh, star of *Gone with the Wind*, her father's favorite film, as he had once told her in passing. Phuong had seen the film on a pirated videotape, and was seduced immediately by the glamour, beauty, and sadness of Scarlett O'Hara, heroine and embodiment of a doomed South. Was it too much to suppose that the ruined Confederacy, with its tragic sense of itself, bore more than a passing similarity to her father's defeated southern Republic and its resentful remnants?

It was easy, then, in the weeks leading to Vivien's arrival, for Phuong to pass her days at home and at work constructing scenarios of a noble, kindly sister, somewhat solemn and sad, but nevertheless gentle and patrician, who would immediately take to her and become the mentor and guide Phuong never had. Her first glimpse of Vivien at the airport only confirmed the appropriateness of such a movie star's name for the young woman who paused at the terminal's glass gates, her eyes hidden behind enormous sunglasses, her lips slightly parted in a glossy pout, pushing a cart loaded with her own weight in crimson luggage. As she jumped and waved to get Vivien's attention, Phuong was thrilled to see that her sister bore utterly no resemblance to the throngs of local people waiting outside to greet the arrivals, hundreds of ordinary folk wearing drab clothes and fanning themselves under the sun.

Even after a week in Saigon, Vivien would appear no more of a native than on the day she arrived, at least in outdoor settings. On the streets, at sidewalk cafés, or hopping into a taxi, she was easily mistaken for a Korean businessman's frazzled wife or a weary Japanese tourist, her frosting of makeup melting under the tropical glare. In certain indoor settings, however, she was clearly the mistress of her domain. This was the case at the restaurant Nam Kha, on the street Dong Khoi, where Phuong had worked as a hostess for the two years since her graduation from college. It was Vivien's idea to treat the family to dinner at Nam Kha, a way to celebrate the halfway point in her vacation and something Phuong would never have suggested, the restaurant's offerings being far more than Phuong or her family could afford.

"But it's a crime, don't you think?" Vivien said, glancing over the entrées. Their table was by the reflecting pool, across from which two young women sat upon a cushioned dais, wearing silken, ethereal *ao dai* and plucking gently at the sixteen strings of the zithers braced upon their laps. "You should be able to eat where you work at least once in your lifetime."

"The real crime is five dollars for morning glory fried in garlic," Mrs. Ly said. She sold silk at the Ben Thanh market and possessed the eyes of an experienced negotiator, smooth and unreadable as the beads of an abacus. "I can buy this for a dollar at the market."

"Look around," Mr. Ly said, his tone impatient. All the other guests were white with the exception of an Indian couple in the corner, the man in a linen suit and the woman in a *salwar kameez*. "These are tourist prices."

"These are foolish prices."

"Price aside, this is a good restaurant," Vivien declared. Her voice was authoritative, the way she must sound in her examination room in Chicago. Not for the first time, Phuong imagined herself in her sister's place, wearing a white coat in a white room, looking out a wall of windows at a haze of white snow. "What do you think?" Vivien nudged her knee. "Too outrageous for you?"

"Not at all!" Phuong hoped that she projected an air of confidence and ease, unlike her brothers. Hanh and Phuc were speechless, their silk-bound menus considerably more handsome than any textbook they owned. "I could get used to this."

"That's the spirit."

The guests at the neighboring table rose, and on the way out, two of them paused beside Phuong, the brunette taking a photograph of the musicians strumming their zithers. "They're just like butterflies," she said in an Australian accent, squinting at the image on her camera. Eavesdropping on them, Phuong was relieved not to be the object of their fascination. "So delicate and tiny."

"I'll bet they never worry about what they eat." Her friend flipped open her compact to inspect her lipstick. "Those dresses look stitched onto them."

Night after night, Phuong had observed the customs of tourists like these, her degree in biology no more than a memory as she opened the doors of Nam Kha with a small bow. Having come to dine on elegantly presented peasant cuisine, the guests were suitably impressed by the Cham statuary, by the Chinese scrolls hanging upon the walls, and by Phuong herself, her slim and petite body sheathed in a golden, formfitting *ao dai*. Sometimes guests would ask to photograph her, requests that were initially flattering but now usually irritating. Still, she could not decline, as her manager had made clear, and so she would force herself to smile and tilt her head, a trellis of hair as black and silky as her trousers falling over her shoulder. Striking this or another pose, Phuong could pretend that she was not a hostess doing a foreigner's bidding, but rather a model, a starlet, her sibling's namesake. What she actually looked like she never knew, for while everyone promised to send her the pictures, no one ever did.

When she arrived, Vivien carried with her a schedule of the sights she wanted to see, complete with estimated travel times via train, bus, car, hydrofoil, or plane. President Clinton had come the year before, his much-celebrated visit reassuring her mother that Vivien could return safely, especially when armed with a US passport and dollar bills. So equipped, Vivien had overcome her father's token resistance and paid for the family during all of their outings. "I'm the doctor, aren't I?" she said. While Phuong was impressed by Vivien's approach, as if vacationing were a job in which to seek promotion, she was not surprised. In the occasional dispatches sent by Vivien's mother, a picture had emerged of an independent young woman, the unmarried pediatrician who had backpacked solo through Western Europe and vacationed in Hawaii, the Bahamas, Rio. Mr. Ly, who made a humble living as a tour guide, reviewed the itinerary and said, "I couldn't have done better myself."

He was a man who rarely praised, except when it came to his first trio of children. His wife had absconded with them after the war, when he had been banished to a New Economic Zone and his mistress had come demanding money. Vivien's mother had been ignorant of the other woman's existence until then, and her response was to flee the country with her three children on a perilous trip by boat. Mr. Ly had learned of their flight in the middle of his five-year sentence, the loss leading to a spell of shock and depression that he had not shaken off until his return to Saigon. Life must move on, his mistress said, so he had divorced Vivien's mother, made his mistress the second Mrs. Ly, and sired three more children. He often compared Phuong with her absent sister, which had cultivated in Phuong a sense of yearning for Vivien but also some undeniable jealousy. A weevil of envy resurfaced nearly every day of Vivien's visit, for her father was behaving completely unlike himself, as if he were also competing at a job, in this case to win Vivien's approval. Without question or criticism, he followed Vivien's plan for visiting temples and cathedrals, shopping malls and museums, beaches and resorts, south through the Mekong Delta, east to Vung Tau, north to Dalat, and, within Saigon, from the dense, cacophonous alleys of the Chinese quarter in Cho Lon to the glamour of downtown's Dong Khoi, where Nam Kha was the most expensive restaurant on the boulevard.

"This is like Saigon in the old days." Mr. Ly smiled fondly, gazing upon the restaurant's velvet draperies and marble pillars. During the war, he had owned a shoe factory, a beach home in Vung Tau, a chauffeured Citroën. Photographs from that time showed a dapper man with pomaded hair and a thin mustache. Now, so far as Phuong could tell, he wore his sadness and defeat in a paunch barely contained by the buttons of a shirt one size too small for him. "L'Amiral on Thai Lap Thanh. La Tour d'Ivoire on Tran Hung Dao. Paprika, with the best paella and sangria. I always used to go to those restaurants."

"Not with me," Mrs. Ly said.

"What do you want to do tomorrow?" Mr. Ly asked Vivien. She refilled his glass from the bottle of Australian merlot and said, "I left it blank on my schedule. I always leave a day or two for surprises."

"Can we go to Dam Sen?" Hanh asked. Phuc nodded vigorously.

"What's that?" Vivien refilled her own glass.

"An amusement park," Phuong said. She was drinking lemonade, as were her mother and brothers. "It's not far from here."

"I worked in one when I was sixteen," Vivien said. "That was a crazy summer."

"We can save Dam Sen for later," Mr. Ly said. "Since you've seen where your sister works, let me take you on one of my tours tomorrow."

"One hundred percent." Vivien raised her glass, using the classic toast he had taught her.

He clinked his glass against hers, gazed upon his sons affectionately, and said, "Yours is a lucky generation."

"I wouldn't say we were so lucky," Phuong said.

"You've never appreciated what you have." Her father waved his hand over the meal and Phuong squeezed her glass, bracing to hear the stories of her parents one more time. "You want to talk about bad luck? After the Americans abandoned us and the Communists sent me to the labor camp, we ate roots and manioc to live. There were worms in the rice, which was mostly water. People caught dysentery or malaria or dengue fever like the common cold and just died. It was amazing we had blood left for the leeches."

"It wasn't so much better at home," Mrs. Ly chimed in. "I sold everything to survive after the war. My sewing machine. The record player you gave me, and the records, too."

"The dumbest part was the confessions." Mr. Ly stared into his glass, as if all the lessons learned in the labor camp, once distilled, merely served to fill it. "Every week I had to come up with a different way to criticize myself for being a capitalist. I wrote enough pages for a whole autobiography, but every chapter said the same thing."

Phuong sighed, but Vivien was listening intently, chin cupped in her hand. "There's something I've always wanted to know." When their father looked up, Vivien said, "Why give your children with your other wife our names?"

This was the question Phuong had never asked, fearing the answer she always suspected, that she and her brothers were no more than regrets born into flesh. Vivien's forthrightness, however, did not appear to surprise or daunt their father, who merely raised his glass and said, "If you hadn't come back to see me, I would have understood. But I knew you would come back to see the one I named after you."

Vivien glanced at Phuong, who maintained a stoic expression. After all, it wasn't Vivien's fault their father behaved the way he did, playing favorites and pitying himself. "So here I am," Vivien said. She returned her father's gaze and clinked her glass against his. "And here's to us."

"One hundred percent," Mr. Ly said.

For all the years that Mr. Ly had worked as a tour guide, he had never asked Phuong to accompany him on one of his trips. Although she had never wanted to go, she realized the next morning on the tour bus that she would like to have been asked. Vivien did not seem to appreciate their father's special regard for her, or her fortune in even being a tourist on this day, the boys left behind at school and Phuong's mother busy at the Ben Thanh market. Instead, Vivien focused her attention on the crowded conditions of the aging bus, whispering complaints into Phuong's ear about the long-haired, budget-minded backpackers who jammed the thinly cushioned seats and made their father's company a success. Then, embraced by clammy weather once they stepped off the air-conditioned bus at Ben Dinh, Vivien could only mutter that this was not exactly her idea of fun.

"I don't even like camping," Vivien said as the sisters trailed behind the other tourists, winding their way through the eucalyptus trees and bamboo groves where the fabled tunnels of Cu Chi were preserved. "I'd rather be in a shopping mall or a museum, but even the museums don't have air-conditioning here."

"Father wants you to see him at work," Phuong said patiently. "He's good at what he does."

"Don't tell him I said anything, okay? I don't want to hurt his feelings."

"So we have a secret?" Phuong teased.

"Sisters have to have secrets," Vivien said. "Oh my God. What is it? Thirty-four degrees?"

"This isn't so bad. It's not even that hot."

"I'm being bitten. I can feel it. Look at my legs!"

Vivien's shins and thighs were studded with the pale bumps of fresh bites and the red kernels of fermenting ones. For a pediatrician and seasoned traveler, Vivien had proved woefully incapable of caring for her body. While Phuong wore gloves extending to her upper arms and nylons underneath her jeans, her sister wore T-shirts that exposed her bra straps and shorts that were sometimes so brief they revealed the waistband and thong of her panties. Despite her bared skin, Vivien neglected to use mosquito repellent and complained whenever the weather was hot, which was, according to her, nearly every second of the day and night. Her sister's vulnerability was alternately a source of annoyance and endearment to Phuong, rendering Vivien less intimidating and perhaps more deserving of the secret Phuong longed to entrust, what she had never told her family and what only Vivien could understand.

"This, ladies and gentlemen, a *punji* trap." Mr. Ly spoke in English, beckoning for the group to halt. The two dozen tourists, all Westerners, stepped close to the bamboo trapdoor. He spun it on its hinge until it was vertical, revealing a pit as deep as a grave and as long as a coffin, a dozen sharp wooden stakes embedded in the earth. "Step on trapdoor, you fall in."

After a couple of tourists took photographs, Mr. Ly waved the group forward. He wore a short-sleeved white shirt and gray slacks with polished brown leather shoes, whereas at home he typically lounged in shorts and, perhaps, an undershirt. What was strangest to Phuong was seeing her father joke and chat with the tourists. Whenever he spoke to Phuong at home, it was mostly to call for another beer, or to have her fetch him his cigarettes, or to request a particular dish for dinner.

"And this, an original tunnel." Mr. Ly stopped and pointed at a square hole the size of a sheet of paper, covered with a wood board and a scattering of leaves at the foot of a eucalyptus tree. "Here, guerrillas live for years and attack Americans anytime."

The tourists were almost all Americans, but this history did not seem to offend them. Instead, they seemed fascinated, raising their cameras as he lifted the board to show the narrow, dark entrance. In the distance, from the shooting range, a machine gun fired a burst of rounds, each bullet costing a dollar, according to their father. Phuong was bemused at how these tourists would want to spend their money and their day here, instead of at the beach, or at a fancy restaurant, or in a hammock at a rustic riverside café. The reason for such behavior, her father said, was that the foreign tourists knew only one thing about this country, the war. These tunnels, then, were a must-see on their itineraries.

"Later we see new tunnels, made big just for you. Last time an American go in this one, he can't get out. He too fat!" To illustrate his point, Mr. Ly extended his arms and joined his hands, creating a large hoop in the air. "Anyone want to try?"

The tourists grinned and shook their heads, the smallest of them as tall as Phuong's father. Phuong was afraid he might call on her to slide into the tunnel, but when no one volunteered, her father scowled and raised his fist. "This is how we win our victory!" he cried. A camera flashed. "We reunite our country through courage and sacrifice!"

Two more cameras flashed as their father held his pose.

"Did he just say what I think he said?" Vivien whispered.

"He doesn't really mean it. It's only an act."

But Phuong suspected that for the tourists, act was fact. Foreigners that they were, they could not tell the difference between a Communist and a man the Communists had exiled to a New Economic Zone. In a few days, or a week, or two weeks, they would leave, their most vivid memory about this day being the funny experience of crawling on their knees through a tunnel, with a vague memory of the passionate little tour guide and his somewhat quirky English. We're all the same to them, Phuong understood with a mix of anger and shame—small, charming, and forgettable. She was worried her sister might see her in this way as well, but when her father waved the tourists onward and Vivien followed, she appeared to be concerned only with brushing away the small cloud of mosquitoes hovering around her.

On Vivien's penultimate night in Saigon, she and her father drank four flasks of milky rice wine at a Chinese restaurant in Cho Lon. After returning home, he went for a walk with his wife to clear his intoxicated head while Hanh and Phuc settled down on the blanketed floor of the living room, their bed next to the motorbikes. Upstairs, after Vivien closed the door to the room that Phuong shared with her parents, she pulled one of her crimson suitcases out from underneath Phuong's narrow bed. The suitcase had been loaded with gifts from Vivien and her mother, from jeans and shirts to medicines and makeup, even shampoo and conditioner that had been bottled in the United States and were hence more valuable than the same brand bottled in a local plant. Now the suitcase was packed with souvenirs, a porcelain doll in a silk *ao dai* for Vivien's mother, hand-carved teak replicas of cyclos for her brothers, a bottle of rice wine with a cobra floating in it for her stepfather, and, for her friends, T-shirts emblazoned with Ho Chi Minh's avuncular face. But when Vivien opened the suitcase, she took out neither these mementos nor her own belongings. Instead, after rummaging underneath them, she dug out a small pink bag, somewhat crumpled from its journey, and presented it to Phuong.

"I've got one last thing for you, little sister," Vivien said. "I wasn't sure I should give it to you, but I thought I'd come prepared."

Printed on the bag in cursive writing was *Victoria's Secret*. Inside were a black lace brassiere and black lace panties, a wispy thong rather than one of the scratchy, full-bottomed cotton affairs that Phuong's mother bought for her in packages of a dozen.

"I can't wear these!" Phuong said, blushing. "They're scandalous!"

"Go on, try them on." Vivien pulled the nearly nonexistent panties from the bag and pressed them into Phuong's hands. "I can't imagine you in those granny things you have."

For a moment, Phuong hesitated. But Vivien was her sister and a doctor, and there was no need to be shy. She quickly stripped off her rayon pajamas and her cotton underwear, and just as quickly slipped on the brassiere and panties. Vivien nodded approvingly and said, "Now you look sexy. Some boy's going to be very lucky to see you in those."

"My mother and father would never let me wear these." Phuong hesitated, but then reached for the hand mirror hanging from a nail in the wall. The touch of lace against her skin and the glimpses of her nearly nude body, draped so provocatively, were thrilling. "Only naughty girls would wear this."

"It's time for you to be bad," Vivien said, yawning. "My God, you're twenty-three! You don't even want to know what I was doing when I was twenty-three."

Even after Phuong had put her pajamas back on, she could still see how she looked in the hand mirror, the flashes of skin against the strip of gossamer fabric. She drew the curtain separating her side of the room from her parents' and slipped into bed with Vivien, who had put away the suitcase and donned her own pajamas. Lying there, arm by arm, she sensed that her sister's gift had endowed their relationship with even more intimacy and trust.

"What's the first thing you'll do in Chicago? Call your mother?"

"Take a long drive by myself. I miss my car."

"I don't even know anyone who owns a car."

Vivien stared at the ceiling fan, stirring the hot air of a typically humid night. The open window allowed in only the merest of breezes.

"Can I tell you a secret?" Vivien said.

"You already told me."

"What?"

"A secret." When Phuong turned her head, she could see into Vivien's ear, the canal small and dark. "At Cu Chi."

"I guess I did." Vivien scratched a bite on her neck. "I thought I would come here and I would love my father."

"You don't love him?" Phuong propped her head on her hand. "Or you didn't love him?"

"It's easy for you to love him." Vivien sighed. "It's easy for him to love me. That's the way it should be. He remembers me. I don't remember him. Can you love someone you don't remember? Can you love someone you don't know?"

"I'm not sure." A burst of cackling and laughter came from the alley outside, the neighborhood's old ladies sitting on their thresholds, gossiping before bedtime. "But I know he's not easy to love."

"A woman can't fall in love with a man for whom she feels sorry. Can she?"

"I've never fallen in love with anyone, so I don't know." The screech of the metal gate that was the living room's front door announced their father's return. "But you're saying it wrong. You're not falling in love, you just want to love him."

"You know what my mother told me when I said I was going to Vietnam?" Vivien paused. "Your father's only going to break your heart, too."

Then Vivien rolled over on her side to face the wall, where a green gecko clung patiently to the plaster. The stairs creaked as Mr. and Mrs. Ly ascended, the discordant notes together composing a coda to Phuong's day so familiar only Vivien's arrival made her aware of it. Her sister's presence in Phuong's bed and the caress of the lace on her skin sharpened the dull pencil of Phuong's perceptions, allowing her to write in her mind with ever-increasing precision the outline of the characters in her life. None was drawn more clearly than her father, whom she pitied and, even worse, did not respect. If he were only an adulterer and a playboy, then there would be cause for resentment, but he was in decline, a failure without even the glamour of decadence and bad behavior. This was a matter of sufficient sadness and embarrassment so that when her father's shadow appeared in the doorway, Phuong turned on her side as well. There, pressed into her sister's back under the weight of a humid night, she discovered that even lying down Vivien had broken into a sweat.

At the amusement park the next morning, Mr. Ly photographed his children at the entry gates with a disposable camera, a gift from his ex-wife, delivered by Vivien. After Vivien paid for the family's fares, Hanh and Phuc seized the lead, the former tugging on his mother's hand. They picked their way through raucous troops of elementary school boys and girls, a battalion in red shirts and caps. A monorail traversed the park above the keen crowds, and in the distance, a roller coaster rumbled. One exhibition hall soon caught Phuong's attention, its curious English name being the "Ice Lantern." On a billboard outside, brightly colored photos depicted glacial facsimiles of the Eiffel Tower, the Taj Mahal, and other man-made wonders of the world, lit in a rainbow of neon. "Let's save this for later," she said, "when we need to cool down."

"Good plan," said Vivien, fanning herself with the park brochure.

After driving the bumper cars at Hanh's and Phuc's request, Mrs. Ly insisted on visiting the Japanese orchid garden. Several young couples posed for wedding photographs in different corners, the veiled brides in Western wedding gowns and the grooms in white tuxedos, red roses pinned to their lapels. Mrs. Ly cooed over the spectacle, but Hanh and Phuc rolled their eyes and asked Vivien if the next destination could be the Ferris wheel, rotating slowly above the water slides. It was Mrs. Ly who clambered into one cabin of the Ferris wheel with the boys, while Mr. Ly declined to join his daughters in another cabin, claiming acrophobia. As they ascended, Vivien studied the scenery from the barred window on her side, below which someone had drawn on the blue wall the stick figure of a girl with a mop of hair, fingers flashing a V. Phuong peeked over her shoulder, her breath tickling a strand of hair on Vivien's ear. Vivien tucked away the hair and pointed toward the roller coaster climbing slowly into view, an upside-down caterpillar with dozens of human arms wiggling in the air. "I worked on a ride like that," Vivien said. "All my friends found jobs at the park so we could meet boys."

"Did you find a boyfriend?" Phuong leaned a shoulder against her sister's arm. She hadn't told Vivien that she was still wearing her gift, delighting in it like a child with a new and magical toy. "Was he handsome?"

"Rod was cute. He'd give me rides home, and we'd go on one of the side streets around my house, park, and . . . kiss. I don't suppose you've done that?"

"Not yet."

"You haven't found any boys you like?"

"I don't want any attachments," Phuong said firmly. "I don't want anyone holding me back."

"From what?"

At the center of the park was a lake the size of a saucer, crumbs of paddleboats floating on its surface. Jutting into the lake was their noon destination, a restaurant in the shape of a dragon's head, dividing the waters as Vivien's departure tomorrow would divide the world once more into those who stayed and those who left.

"Can I tell you a secret now?"

Vivien smiled. "Sure."

Phuong searched for the words to say what she had never told anyone before, how one day she, too, would leave, for Saigon was boring and the country itself not big enough for the desires in her heart. "I want to be like you," Phuong said, gripping her sister's hands in her own. "I want to go to America and be a doctor and help people. I don't want to spend my life waiting on people. I want to be waited on. I want to travel anywhere I want, anytime I want. I want to come back here and know I can leave. If I stay here I'll marry some boy with no future and live with his family and have two children too soon and sleep in a room where I can touch both walls at the same time. I don't think I can stand it, I really don't. Haven't you ever felt this way?"

"Oh God," Vivien said, looking up at the ceiling of the cabin. Phuong had hoped for enthusiasm and would have settled for reluctance, confusion, or condescension, but she was not prepared for the panic on her sister's face. "I told her she should have told all of you the truth."

The roller coaster plunged down the tracks, the passengers screaming. When Vivien shifted her weight and pulled her hands free, her arm peeled away from Phuong's shoulder with a moist suck of sound, the air no cooler than down below.

"Who are you talking about?"

"My mother." Vivien took a deep breath and looked once more through the barred windows. "Did you know that when she came to the States, she told the government she was twenty-five?"

"So?" A drop of sweat trickled down the small of Phuong's back.

"She was thirty."

"I can see a woman doing that."

"My mother also told the government she was a widow." Vivien turned back to meet Phuong's gaze. "She wasn't telling the truth when she told our father I was a doctor."

Phuong blinked. "You're not a doctor?"

"I'm a receptionist without a job. I was let go the month before I came here. My mother and my stepfather do not own a house in the suburbs. They live in a condo in West Tulsa. And my mother does not own the Nice Nail Beauty Salon. She works for it as a beautician."

"Then why tell us you were a doctor?"

"Because you all wanted to know how much I made a month, and what I paid on my mortgage, and how much my car cost. It was easier just to answer than to say I wasn't a doctor. But just so you know, that whole story about me being a pediatrician was my mother's idea, not mine." The cabin had reached its zenith, an elephant chained by its ankle visible far below, a windup toy tottering back and forth. "My mother also told me not to date my boss, especially if he's married."

"Your boss? What's he got to do with this?"

"He said it wasn't me, it was the economy," Vivien cried. "Have you ever heard anything so stupid?"

"No," Phuong said. "No one's ever broken up with me before."

"It happens to everybody." Vivien's eyes moistened. "So I thought I'd come here. A stupid reason, isn't it?"

"I thought you came here to see us."

"That, too."

"Where's all the money coming from?" Phuong could not tabulate how much her sister had spent, but she knew it was in the thousands of dollars. Just the gift envelopes alone that Vivien had distributed on her first night in Saigon held six hundred-dollar bills for Mr. and Mrs. Ly, with two more for Phuong and one each for her brothers. "All the dinners and tickets? The trips to Dalat and Vung Tau?"

"In America, they pay you extra when they fire you. Even receptionists get a nice check from big companies." Vivien fumbled in her purse as their cabin continued its descent. "I also have credit cards. I don't mind spending money. I wanted to show you a good time. You've never been anywhere."

The park's most prominent landmark loomed before them, a mountain painted an alluvial red, hollow and metallic. "It doesn't matter," Phuong said. None of it did, neither the lies nor the fact that Vivien had everything, even Phuong's name, which she didn't care to use. "You don't have to be a doctor to sponsor me."

"Where are my tissues?" Vivien wiped her tears away with her hands.

"I won't bother you." Phuong touched Vivien on the arm, sticky with perspiration. Their cabin was nearing the platform. "I'll find a job. I'll take care of myself. I'll take care of you."

Vivien snapped her purse shut, still crying. "I'm sorry, Phuong. When I return, I'm putting my life back together. I've got to pay off four credit cards and my student loans and hope my house won't be taken from me."

"But—"

"I won't have time to worry about a little sister." Now it was Vivien who seized Phuong's hands with her own tear-dampened ones. "Can you understand that? Please?"

When the attendant opened the door, their father was waiting, disposable camera held to his eye, his wife standing behind him with the boys. The Ferris wheel rotated at its measured pace, slow enough for them to step out, Vivien first. A week later their father would develop the photograph, but it would take Phuong a moment to examine the laminated picture before she remembered what was absent underneath the clear plastic. Vivien was visible in the doorway, eyes moist and makeup smudged, but by an accident of timing or composition Phuong herself could not be seen.

While it had taken Vivien twenty-seven years to mail her first letter home, it took her only a month for the second missive. Phuong returned one evening from Nam Kha to find her parents and brothers clustered around the table in the living room, sifting through a stack of pictures that Vivien had enclosed. A smiling and cheerful Mr. Ly waved the letter at Phuong, a single sheet that she read sitting on the arm of the couch. The letter recounted Vivien's wonderful memories, dining on a floating restaurant on the Saigon River, being fitted for a custom-made *ao dai*, riding on a pony cart around Lake Xuan Huong in Dalat, with the best day her arrival and the worst her departure. *I looked out the window of the airplane until I couldn't see the country anymore*, she wrote. *Everything's so green. The moment the clouds covered it, all I wanted was to return*. And so the letter went, her sister's hypocrisy making Phuong so ill that it was all she could do not to tear the letter in half.

"Tomorrow I want you to have these pictures laminated," Mr. Ly said, sorting through the photographs Vivien had sent. "We'll make an album from them."

"What for?" Phuong said, tossing the letter onto the table.

"What do you mean, what for?" Mr. Ly was incredulous. "So that we'll have something to remember her by until she comes back."

Phuong studied her father as he sat on the couch, surrounded by her mother and brothers, clutching the photographs as if they were equal to the hundred-dollar bills Vivien had given him. For the first time in her life she felt pity for him, certain that it was not just her father who would break his daughter's heart, but the daughters who would one day break his. She contemplated telling him this truth, that Vivien was never going to return, and that one day, perhaps not soon, but eventually, Phuong would leave as well, for a world where she could fall in love with someone she didn't know. It was merely a matter of momentum, and she now knew how to begin.

By nine the next morning she was alone in the house, the boys gone to school, her parents at work. She wore her sister's gift, and over the lace donned a blouse and Capri pants. It would be best, she thought, to do what needed to be done outdoors, and so she placed a stool by the living room gate and a tin bucket on the pavement of the alley. When she opened the envelope of photographs, the first picture she saw featured her father and Vivien shivering in the Ice Lantern at the amusement park, their last stop that day. In the foyer, an attendant had handed them polyester parkas, hooded, knee-length, and in neon hues of yellow, pink, orange, and green. Even with the parkas, stepping from the foyer into the Ice Lantern itself was a shock, for it was in essence an enormous refrigerator, an echoing hall that offered a walking tour of the world's tourist landmarks, rendered as ice sculptures no taller than a man's height. Dazzling neon lights in the same spectrum of color as the parkas illuminated the sculptures, the scurrying crowds, and a pair of long chutes, also carved from ice, down which shrieking children slid.

"This is weird," Vivien had said, hunching her shoulders from the cold as she stood before a miniature version of London's Tower Bridge. It was in front of this bridge that Vivien and her father posed for the photograph, not far from the frozen pyramids of Egypt and the rimy Sphinx. While Phuong aimed Vivien's camera, father and daughter wrapped their arms around each other's waists. Phuong had taken the picture mechanically, not paying much attention to the small digital image after it flashed up on the camera's screen. But now, holding the photograph as she sat on the stool, she could focus on its details. With their hoods over their heads, only her father's and sister's pale, triangular faces were visible, two white petals floating on lily pads of neon green. In the Ice Lantern's glow, her sister's face looked more like her father's than her own, the symmetry rendering clear what Phuong could now say. Their father loved Vivien more than her.

The photograph ignited easily when Phuong lit it with a match. After she dropped the photo into the bucket, she watched it curl up and shrivel, remembering how Vivien had approached her after she took the picture and tried to make amends. "I never thought I'd say this here," Vivien said, smiling as she clasped Phuong's hand, "but I'm cold." Even a month later, Phuong could feel the chilliness, and how she had shivered and turned away toward Egypt's crystalline sand. She fed the fire with more photos and their heat warmed her, two dozen others disappearing until only one was left, of Vivien and Phuong at the airport on the morning of Vivien's departure, Vivien with her arm around Phuong's shoulder and flashing a V sign with her fingers.

Unlike her sister, Phuong was not smiling. Their father had forced her to wear an *ao dai* for Vivien's departure, and she looked serious and grim in its silk confines. Hers was the expression that older people of an earlier generation usually adopted as they stood before the camera, picture-taking a rare and ceremonious occasion reserved for weddings and funerals. The photograph flared when she touched it with fire, Vivien's features melting before her own, their faces vanishing in flame. After the last embers from this photograph and the others had died, Phuong rose and scattered their ashes. She was about to turn and enter the house when a gust of wind surged down the alley, catching the ashes and blowing them away. A flurry rose above the neighboring roofs, and she couldn't help pausing to admire for a moment the clear and depthless sky into which the ashes vanished, an inverted blue bowl of the finest crystal, covering the whole of Saigon as far as her eyes could see.

READ ON FOR TWO ESSAYS BY VIET THANH NGUYEN.

The first article originally appeared
in the *Financial Times* (UK) Life & Arts section
on February 3, 2017.

The second article originally appeared
in the *Los Angeles Times* Jacket Copy section
on April 14, 2017.

On Being a Refugee,
an American—and a Human Being

The Pulitzer Prize–winning novelist and
Vietnam War refugee reflects on American identity

I am a refugee, an American, and a human being, which is important to proclaim, as there are many who think these identities cannot be reconciled. In March 1975, as Saigon was about to fall, or on the brink of liberation, depending on your point of view, my humanity was temporarily put into question as I became a refugee.

My family lived in Ban Me Thuot, famous for its coffee and for being the first town overrun by communist invasion. My father was in Saigon on business and my mother had no way to contact him. She took my ten-year-old brother and four-year-old me and we walked 184 km to the nearest port in Nha Trang (I admit to possibly being carried). At least it was downhill. At least I was too young, unlike my brother, to remember the dead paratroopers hanging from the trees. I am grateful not to remember the terror and the chaos that must have been involved in finding a boat. We made it to Saigon and reunited with my father, and, a month later, when the communists arrived, repeated the mad scramble for our lives. That summer we arrived in America.

I came to understand that in the United States, land of the fabled American dream, it is un-American to be a refugee. The refugee embodies fear, failure, and flight. Americans of all kinds believe that it is impossible for an American to become a refugee, although it is possible for refugees to become Americans and in that way be elevated one step closer to heaven.

To become a refugee means that one's country has imploded, taking with it all the things that protect our humanity: a functional government, a mostly non-murderous police force, a reliable drinking water and food supply, an efficient sewage system (do not underestimate how important a sewage system is to your humanity; refugees know that their subhuman status as the waste of nations is confirmed by having to live in their own waste).

I was luckier than many refugees, but I still remain scarred by my experience. After I arrived in the refugee camp set up at Fort Indiantown Gap, Pennsylvania, at four years old, I was taken away from my parents and sent to live with a white sponsor family. The theory, I think, was that my parents would have an easier time of working if they didn't have to worry about me. Or maybe there was no sponsor willing to take all of us. Regardless, being taken away from my family was simply another sign of how my life was no longer in my hands, or those of my parents. My life was in the hands of strangers, and I was fortunate that they were kind, even if to this day I still remember howling as I was taken from my parents.

THE REFUGEES

Like the homeless, refugees are living embodiments of a disturbing possibility: that human privileges are quite fragile, that one's home, family, and nation are one catastrophe away from being destroyed. As the refugees cluster in camps; as they dare to make a claim on the limited real estate of our conscience—we deny we can be like them and many of us do everything we can to avoid our obligations to them.

The better angels of our nature have always told us that morality means opening our doors, helping the helpless, sharing our material wealth. The reasons we come up with to deny doing such things are rationalizations. We have wealth to share with refugees, but we would rather spend it on other things. We are capable of living with foreigners and strangers, but they make us uncomfortable, and we do not want to be uncomfortable. We fear that strangers will kill us, so we keep them out.

Our fate as refugees is controlled by the strategies of the men who command the bombers. In my case, the US dropped more bombs on Vietnam, Laos, and Cambodia during the Vietnam War than it did all of Europe during the Second World War. This played a role in creating refugees, and because of American guilt and anticommunist feeling, the US government took in 150,000 Vietnamese refugees in 1975. It authorized the admission of several hundred thousand more, and other Southeast Asian refugees, in the subsequent decade. What the US did exceeded what Southeast Asian countries did, which was to deny entry to the "boat people" or contain them in camps until they could find a host country like the United States. Accepting these refugees was proof that the US was paying its debt to its South Vietnamese allies, and the refugees became reminders that life under communism was horrible. We were expected to be grateful for our rescue from such a life, and many of us were and are thankful.

"But I was also one of those unfortunate cases who could not help but wonder whether my need for American charity was due to my having first been the recipient of American aid," or so I wrote in my novel *The Sympathizer*. I am a bad refugee, you see, who can't help but see that my good fortune is a stroke of bureaucratic luck and the racial politics of the United States, where Asians are considered model minorities. If I was Haitian in the 1970s and 1980s, I would not have been admitted as a refugee, because I was black and poor. If I was Central American today, I would not be admitted as a refugee, even though the US has destabilized the region in the past through supporting dictatorial regimes and creating the conditions for the drug economy and drug wars. I am a bad refugee because I insist on seeing the historical reasons that create refugees and the historical reasons for denying refugee status to certain populations.

Central Americans are categorized instead by the United States as immigrants, which suspends questions over the influence of American policy on their countries of origin. The immigrant is that foreigner who has proceeded through the proper channels. The immigrant is the one who wants to come, unlike the refugee, who is forced to come. The im migrant, as contrasted to the refugee, is awesome. The im-migrant, in turn, makes America awesome. Or great. I forget the right word. In any case, here are the famous words on the Statue of Liberty:

> *"Give me your tired, your poor,*
> *Your huddled masses yearning to*
> *breathe free,*
> *The wretched refuse of your*
> *teeming shore.*
> *Send these, the homeless, tempest-tost*
> *to me,*
> *I lift my lamp beside the golden door!"*

Except that this has not always been true. The current xenophobia in American society that is directed against ref-ugees and their cousins, undocumented immigrants, and even against legal immigrants, has deep roots. Inasmuch as America has been built by immigrants and is welcoming to foreigners, it has also been built on genocide, slavery, and colonialism.

These two aspects of America are contradictory but both are true at the same time, as they are true of the other liberal democracies of the west. So it is that in the US, where 51 per-cent of billion-dollar start-ups were founded by immigrants, and all of the 2016 Nobel Prize winners are immigrants, the country has periodically turned on its immigrants. Beginning in 1882, the United States banned Chinese immigrants. The excuse was that the Chinese were an economic, moral, sexual, and hygienic threat to white Americans. In retrospect, these reasons seem ridiculous, particularly given how well Chinese Americans have integrated into American society. These reasons should make us aware of how laughable contemporary fears about Muslims are—these fears are as irrational as the racism directed against the Chinese. Various other legal acts effectively ended non-white immigration to the country by 1924, and while the door would slowly creak open with the repeal of the Chinese Exclusion Act in 1943 (when 105 Chinese were permitted to enter annually), the United States would not embrace open immigration until 1965's Immigration Act.

The contemporary US has been defined by that act, with large numbers of Asian and Latino immigrants coming in and reshaping what America is (and for the better; without immigration from non-white countries, American food would be as terrible as that of pre-immigration England). But the prejudice remains. It emerges in the feeling against undocumented immigrants. Those who oppose them say we should give preference to documented immigrants, but I suspect that once the undocumented have been kicked out, these rational people will start speaking about how there are too many immigrants in general.

In truth, my own family is an example of the model minority that could be used to rebut such an argument. My parents became respectable merchants. My brother went to Harvard seven years after arriving in the States with no

English. I won the Pulitzer Prize. We could be put on a poster touting how refugees make America great. And we do. But it shouldn't take this kind of success to be welcomed. Even if refugees, undocumented immigrants, and legal immigrants are not all potential billionaires, that is no reason to exclude them. Even if their fate is to be the high-school dropout and the fast-food cashier, so what? That makes them about as human as the average American, and we are not about to deport the average American (are we?).

The average American, or European, who feels that refugees or immigrants threaten their jobs does not recognize that the real culprits for their economic plight are the corporate interests and individuals that want to take the profits and are perfectly happy to see the struggling pitted against each other. The economic interests of the unwanted and the fearful middle class are aligned—but so many can't see that because of how much they fear the different, the refugee, the immigrant. In its most naked form, this is racism. In a more polite form, it takes the shape of defending one's culture, where one would rather remain economically poor but ethnically pure. This fear is a powerful force, and I admit to being afraid of it.

Then I think of my parents, who were younger than me when they lost nearly everything and became refugees. I can't help but remember how, after we settled in San Jose, California, and my parents opened a Vietnamese grocery store in the rundown downtown, a neighboring store put a sign up in its window: "Another American driven out of business by the Vietnamese." But my parents did not give in to fear, even though they must have been afraid. And I think of my son, nearly the age I was when I became a refugee, and while I do not want him to be afraid, I know he will be. What is important is that he have the strength to overcome his fear. And the way to overcome fear is to demand the America that should be, and can be, the America that dreams the best version of itself.

In Praise of Doubt and Uselessness

Almost exactly twenty years ago, I arrived in Los Angeles in the month of June. I had received my doctorate from UC Berkeley in May and had turned twenty-six in February. That summer, I found a small apartment in Silver Lake and began preparing for a new career as a professor at USC. I look back on myself with bemusement and sympathy, for there were many things I did not know when I was twenty-six. My naiveté protected me when I sat down to write at my small kitchen table and in that hot, stifling, first summer in Los Angeles began a short-story collection. If I had known that it would take me seventeen years to finish that collection, and three more years to publish it, perhaps I never would have even begun.

But ignorance can sometimes—not always, but sometimes—be as beneficial as knowledge. Ignorance is beneficial when we are aware of it. In my case, to paraphrase a former Secretary of Defense, I knew what I did not know, and I knew that I wanted to know it, but I did not know how to know it. I knew that I wanted to write fiction, and I knew that I wanted to produce innovative scholarship, but I did not know how to do either of those things. I also knew that universities did not reward ignorance, or the confession of ignorance, and so I kept my ignorance to myself and pretended that I knew what I was doing.

That successful act of fiction led to receiving tenure, six years later. To receive tenure, I did what I knew how to do. I became an academic professional and wrote an academic book, which was what I was hired for as a scholar. In my naiveté, I had told myself that once I wrote that book and achieved the freedom of tenure, I would write fiction. It would just take a couple of years to finish that short-story collection, and then it would be sold and published and win prizes and I would be famous. I vaguely knew, but didn't really understand, how much writing would demand from me, how much it would dismantle me as a professional, much to my own grief but ultimately for my own betterment as a writer and a scholar.

For the next nine years, I learned about grief as I worked on that damned short-story collection. I did not know what I was doing, and what I also did not know, facing my computer screen and a white wall, slowly turning pale, was that I was becoming a writer. Becoming a writer was partly a matter of acquiring technique, but it was just as importantly a matter of the spirit and a habit of the mind. It was the willingness to sit in that chair for thousands of hours, receiving only occasional and minor recognition, enduring the grief of writing in the belief that somehow, despite my ignorance, something transformative was taking place.

It was an act of faith, and faith would not be faith if it was not hard, if it was not a test, if it was not an act of willful ignorance, of believing in something that can neither be predicted nor proved by any scientific metric.

At the same time, I was testing myself as a scholar. I began work on another scholarly book. Its evolution would run parallel to my fiction writing, and if I had known that this scholarly book on the memories of the Vietnam War would take fourteen years to be published, I probably would have chosen another subject. One reason it took so long was that it investigated literature, film, museums, memorials, politics, philosophy, and history. But even more challenging for me was that I wanted the book to be as much a creative work as a critical work, just as I wanted my fiction to be as critical as it was creative. But I didn't know how to do this, and no one could teach me this, and it took the discipline of sitting in a chair for countless hours over twenty years before I could even approach bringing together the critical and the creative.

I've told this story about my ignorance and my naiveté, of my struggles and my doubts, because most readers are only aware of the final product of a writer or scholar's efforts. That final product, the book, appears brimming with confidence and knowledge. Confidence and knowledge, and the "metrics" of evaluation and advancement that saturate our lives in schools, corporations, and bureaucracies obscure the mysterious, intuitive, and slow—sometimes very slow—ways in which art and scholarship often operate. At a time in which the demand for productivity and the measuring of outputs has increased in the university—indeed, everywhere—it is important to acknowledge how much of what is crucial in the work that matters to us, no matter what our field, can neither be quantified nor accelerated.

In my case, someone looking at me might see that I have published three books in the last three years and think that I am fast-paced and prolific, without realizing that it took twenty years of slow—very slow—thinking and arduous labor to produce those books. What is valuable about my worlds of the arts and humanities is that they create spaces for this type of slow thinking. And by this I mean that we value the arts and humanities not simply for the material possibilities and rewards they may bring, like a Pulitzer Prize. Rather, we should value the arts and humanities for their privileging of the mystery and intuition that makes moments of revelation and innovation possible.

I think of the novelist Haruki Murakami, who compares writing a novel to digging a hole through deep rock to reach a source of water. To access mystery and intuition requires hard work and is a gamble, for there is no guarantee that we will find that source of water. We need universities and governments to invest in the arts and humanities so that we can teach students about the importance of mystery and intuition, and the need to take a risk, to gamble on one's beliefs and values. And we need universities and governments to protect and to nurture the artist and the scholar—even if their work takes decades, even if the artist and the scholar are shrouded in obscurity while they carry out their labor, even if the gamble doesn't always pay off.

Of course, my novel *The Sympathizer* is not obscure at the moment because of the Pulitzer Prize. But the novel might just as well *not* have gotten it, might as well have sunken into obscurity because it lacked a prize, even if nothing in the novel was any different for having gotten a prize. The novel's good fortune only changes how people look at the novel, not the novel itself. I think of all the other novels that might have won the prize, or all the novels that didn't win prizes in other years that could have or should have won prizes. Some of those unrecognized novels, as time will show, will be triumphant in literary history. The point is that prizes and all that they symbolize in terms of our taste, our judgment, our vanity, and our prejudices are ephemeral. What we are ignorant of in the present may be what the future will value.

Knowledge of this kind of ignorance leads to humility, and also to the awareness that what may seem useless, because it is not rewarded and recognized, might one day be of the greatest usefulness. Although this kind of seemingly useless work happens in the sciences, the burden of uselessness falls with greater weight on the arts and humanities in a world that increasingly values usefulness. When I became an English and ethnic studies double-major as an undergraduate twenty-seven years ago, I took a risk in studying things that a good number of people might think are useless. Perhaps my own parents, refugee shopkeepers who never went to college and who worked twelve- to fourteen-hour days nearly every day of the year, thought my studies to be useless. But to my parents' credit, they suppressed any skepticism and supported my possibly useless studies. They were as ignorant as I was about my future, but they had faith in me.

This is what I think so many of us who work in the arts and the humanities hope to receive from our universities, from our government, from sometimes skeptical students and their parents: patience and faith in us as we test the limits of our ignorance, as we pursue what may very well be useless, as we go in search of that mystery and intuition that exist within all of us.

Acknowledgments

*T*hanks to the editors who first printed these stories.
Thanks to all the wonderful people at my publisher, Grove Atlantic, most especially Peter Blackstock, who said these stories were good enough.

Thanks to my father and mother, Joseph and Linda. Refugees in 1954 and again in 1975, they are the most courageous people I know. They saved my life.

Thanks to my older brother, Tung, the original refugee success story. Seven years after arriving in the United States, he went to Harvard. He sets a high standard.

Thanks to Lan Duong, my fellow refugee, writer, and partner. A reader of my every word, she has shared both the suffering and the joy.

Thanks to our son, Ellison, for reminding me of childhood. By the time this book is published, he will be nearly the age that I was when I became a refugee.